Blaugast

Paul Leppin

BLAUGAST

A Novel of Decline

Translated from the German
by Cynthia A. Klima

TWISTED SPOON PRESS
PRAGUE · 2007

Contents

Publisher's Preface

It should be kept in mind that *Blaugast* was published in German posthumously. Two carbon copies of the typescript are deposited in the Leppin archive at the Museum of Czech Literature, housed in Prague's Strahov Monastery. One typescript bears the title: "*Blaugast*. Roman eines Besessenen." [*Blaugast*: A Novel of One Obsessed]. It seems, however, that "*Blaugast*" was a later addition and Leppin had originally titled it "Der Untergang" [The Decline]. The other typescript is titled "*Blaugast*: Roman eines Untergangs." [*Blaugast*: A Novel of Decline]. Yet when a forthcoming announcement was printed in Leppin's last published book, *Prager Rhapsodie*, in 1938, the title was given as "*Blaugast*. Ein Roman aus dem alten Prag" [*Blaugast*: A Novel from Old Prague].

The novel first appeared in German as volume IV in Dierk Hoffmann's comprehensive dissertation on Paul Leppin (University of Basel, 1973). Here it has the subtitle

"Novel of Decline." When Hoffmann finally had *Blaugast* published in 1984, the subtitle became "Ein Roman aus dem alten Prag." When considering which subtitle to use for our edition, we decided on "A Novel of Decline" as the one that better reflects Leppin's intentions. "A Novel from Old Prague" was likely a late change, and made by the publisher at that.

The translator consulted both the Strahov typescripts and Hoffman's 1984 edition. The typescripts contain Leppin's emendations and other curious marks, and given the flimsy state of the carbon paper, they are difficult to read. We are extremely grateful to the Museum of Czech Literature for taking the time to make copies for us. Hoffmann's edition is eminently more accessible and keeps to Leppin's original text save updated orthography. It should be considered a faithful edition and served as the primary source for the translation.

Blaugast

I

The street greeting Blaugast was now quiet; the stormy night had frightened him out of bed, and he left the sultry room to cool his head by wandering aimlessly in the summer rain. The storm's outburst, which had snarled for some time, had finally moved on; a pleasant quiet had descended. At the end of the street, stars rose over work sites, shimmered as if in reconciliation above the piles of bricks and beams haphazardly stacked. A man with a turned-up jacket collar passed in front of him, then turned around while slightly coughing, as if he'd decided to wait. The way he limped, dragging a lamed foot behind him, steering clear of the puddles, seemed familiar to Blaugast. At the corner, where he passed the man, Blaugast glimpsed his face for a moment, how it smirked, shriveled and became pinched in the light of the lantern.

"Schobotzki!" he called in recognition of his schoolmate of a generation ago, a joyful surprise coloring his voice amid the darkness.

Schobotzki stood still. His long arms, holding together his flapping coat, were crossed at a right angle over his chest; the sharp nose between his eyes gave him the profile of a giant bird of prey. His mouth was sensuously large, his eyebrows unkempt, his forehead knotted under the brim of his hat. "It's you!" he said finally, revealing deformed front teeth. "Septima B., the third corner seat near the window. Klaudius Blaugast, the weakling, though a star pupil in German composition . . ." Blaugast well remembered his celebrated smile — a smile somewhere between melancholy and the accursed familiar.

"What have you been doing with yourself?" he asked with a stroke of deliberate cheerfulness — it seemed appropriate in validating the tone he should take with a friend from his schooldays.

With a mistrustful glance, Schobotzki looked past him, into the street.

"I'm going to seed," he said casually. "Step by step. I am rather well acquainted with the terms."

Blaugast remained speechless; uneasiness gathered into a questionable silence. The man chuckled good-naturedly, then wrapped himself up in the collar of his cloak.

"That's part of the idea," he stated, without explaining himself more clearly. "It has to do with the research I'm involved in. Would you like to see my laboratory?"

"Laboratory?" Blaugast weighed the tone of the question pedantically, with care. Something about the hastiness of the invitation took him aback. Uncomfortably, and without knowing the motive, he enunciated the syllables haltingly.

"Laboratory? Are you still preparing those elixirs in the middle of the night?"

Schobotzki's sharp fingers pressed firmly the arm of his companion.

"Are you not a friend of the night? That's surprising. If you would like to learn about yourself, it's more productive to sleep by day and eat breakfast in the evening. Lamplight renders the thoughts of others transparent. Intangibles melt away; banality phosphoresces in the dark. I know no time better for work than between closing time and morning, especially when a storm like tonight's turns everything upside down. Fanaticism of all sorts grows restless. Just around the next corner, I've discovered an establishment for the initiated, for lovers of novels and other unsentimental types. It's not good to be without a guide on such nights. All these emotions and reservations, all the dung the thunderstorm's flushed out of your thick skull, seem to have frightened you. Come with me, you shit-for-brains. Remember that motto from high school, above the lavatory door: *Nemo Germanus navigat solus.* I don't know if it was good Latin, but it sounded convincing."

During Schobotzki's speech, a mix of random naïveté and pathos, Blaugast was surprised to feel an uneasiness come creeping over his skin, a feeling to which he surrendered. He remembered the naked appearance of the street, the golden façade of the schoolhouse sticking up rudely between the dull tenements. Loud merriment throughout the stairwells, an immature clatter, ridicule and smutty adolescent jokes. But there was also something eerie in these memories, a melding of fantasy with the reality of his schooldays. There were the afternoons when streaks of rain hung on the windows, a hail that both soothed and petrified. Muffled instruction frightening one out of unruly intentions, exhaustion swelling one's veins. Or was it fear knocking around those vaulted hallways, scurrying between the pupils' desks, swelling hesitantly in your mouth? — even today, the aftertaste of an underlying cowardice still hung in Blaugast's saliva. He saw the blackboard covered in figures, his comprehension diminishing with each progressively fine stroke; he saw Schobotzki, his claw-like hands clutching the chalk, bowing his thinly-chiseled, prematurely aged head before the authority of the lectern. For a long time this boy had been a sort of classroom idol — he'd coolly dismissed ambition, eccentrically holding fast to the rules of etiquette, which politely offered affected quirks in lieu of cordiality. His cynicism had long remained a fortress, a formidable example to all his awkward companions, friends who savored the sight of his malicious yet reserved face with the reverence of the schoolboys they were. Now, Blaugast was making his way through the pitch-dark streets with this Schobotzki, this crafty character of his boyhood — who'd sold crib sheets at the most tortuous final exams — the hero of the underclassmen, the notorious mentor at St. Stephen Gymnasium. The lamps burned intermittently behind their rain-drenched domes, illuminating only parts of the street. Some of the authority, which an unforgettable eight-hour detention had reinforced in his being, began to rub off, though imperceptibly, on a relationship that was becoming friendly again. Inevitably, the respect that had characterized the atmosphere at school throughout that entire semester reawakened; indeed, back then it had seemed an incontrovertible law. A dependency, fueled by Schobotzki's nature from the very beginning, was released anew through this encounter.

Blaugast pulled down the brim of his hat and buttoned up his jacket with resolve.

"I'm going with you," he announced, brushing aside doubts with a sweep of his hand. "I suppose your laboratory will offer the possibility of a schnapps. What kind of research is it that leaves such frightful consequences?"

Schobotzki menacingly raised his head off his shoulders.

"Biology of atrophy. Science of decay. Are you inter-ested in catastrophes?"

Stunned, Blaugast searched for a platform from which he could observe the train of thought his companion was merely glossing in aphorism without making much of an effort to clarify. He remembered the circumstances that had often left school staff meetings at a loss, how Schobotzki had always managed to force the mentally and physically weak to submit to his rule. From the ranks of the youngest schoolboys still in short pants, he knew how to summon a coterie of underlings to perform errands and miscellaneous services, those who would hawk his postage stamps at the highest price, or go in search of images clipped from advertising posters for his collection. This willingness was more like an explicit slavery, the dimensions of which the teaching staff could only shake their heads at and never manage completely to control. As willing slaves, the boys were exquisitely trained; they stood in ranks at the side of the accused even as devious rumors of maltreatment ran rampant when outsiders incited the adults. All this ran through Blaugast's mind, although it didn't seem to bear any evident relationship to the question that echoed near him, the question that Schobotzki now pleasurably scruti-nized with his tongue: "Are you interested in catastrophes?"

As it would mean mortal embarrassment to succumb

helplessly to the complexities of such things, Blaugast gave his words an unfriendly haste:

"Catastrophes? — What are those?"

Schobotzki, attempting an unpleasant affability, gave a lukewarm laugh.

"Peak performances. Pure unadulterated results. Changes in the rhythm of cell formation. But we're already here. Watch the steps."

An electric bulb, hanging cool and dim under a whitened metal shade, lit a decrepit stairwell. The musty odor of tobacco and sweat came up from the cellar below, the smell of soup and boiled vegetables. A sausage vendor in an apron and linen jacket sat mindlessly behind his vat, an unshaven chin on his tightened fists. Blaugast remained reluctant, standing near the entrance, where a whore in a threadbare woolen scarf leaned unabashed against the frame of the door.

"Our Prima Donna, the beautiful Wanda," Schobotzki informed him. But the look with which the woman returned his impertinence shocked Blaugast.

The cellar's bar, past the swinging glass door, was not overly crowded. They were an unconventional sort of townsfolk who met here like a family, slurping flat brew out of thick glasses and applauding the quartet that had positioned its music stands among the folds of the moth-eaten curtain at the stairs' landing. The stale merriment with which one of them tapped time on a sticky saucer sounded harshly above the quiet of the others, who rigidly stared into what remained of their beer. Hostile murmuring accompanied their entrance as they looked around among the tables and ordered their liquor from the bartender.

A man in a plaid vest, a freshly-healed scar on a hump on his nose, spat contemptuously on the floor; Blaugast pulled up his crisply-ironed pants while taking a seat. The casual elegance of the visitor, who turned his glass with disapproval between his fingers, had incurred the man's displeasure. But Schobotzki winked at him with appeasement, and a nod of the man's head, knowingly obedient, imperceptibly marked the reply. Sylph-like, impudent, affected in manner, Wanda then approached and sat down next to Blaugast.

Almost submissively, she made use of the privilege of her trade; after so many months of serious emotional turmoil, Blaugast took immediate notice. The familiar form of "you" she used with him came forth darkly, roughened by hoarseness. It drew him in; he spontaneously looked at her face, pensively registering what she said to him.

"Why are you so sad?"

Her eyes, serenely cold, flickered like a candle's flame just before its death. Her hair, combed in a pageboy, was dusty and wild, with disorderly split ends. Her breast stiffened under her short-sleeved blouse, which was dotted with bits of food. Blaugast didn't notice. Long-desired words of comfort unexpectedly soothed his nerves, surrounding him entirely in the glimmer of her question. Why was he so sad? The pent-up feelings of the past weeks, when he had stayed in bed lamenting the futility of his tears, an incomprehensible humiliation — all were alleviated with these words.

"Are you hungry, Wanda?"

She accepted his offer with an enthusiasm that earned her a smile as well. Nimbly flaying the slices of sausage, she chattered away.

Suddenly, Schobotzki disappeared without Blaugast's notice. His angular head, which bent forward furtively when Wanda had approached, appeared once again in the corner of the hall where the musicians grated away at their instruments with a listless bravura. His glance, weighted with suspense, noted in amusement that the apathy of his old friend had vanished, his reservations had disappeared amid the woman's gossip. Schobotzki turned his collar up high, shot a sideways glance at the two of them, then groped his way carefully up the steps from cellar to door.

"Your friend's run out on you," Wanda said after a while.

Blaugast nodded absently. In this moment, as if a vision, his room appeared before him, the rumpled bed, the clock on the wall, mocking —

"Where will you sleep?" he suddenly asked. She shrugged her shoulders.

"I don't know. Here or there. I have no place —"

"Come with me. I'm alone in the apartment. And I'm so afraid of the dark."

II

Whenever Blaugast thought back to his youth he fell, almost instinctively, into making comparisons that served only to intensify any jealous dislike into hatred. He'd turned forty before it gradually dawned on him that the more resounding form of his worldly ties arose only from a particular way of experiencing the Beyond. He'd long thought that the inventive manner with which his acquaintances came to terms with themselves, and with others, was a pose, a clever technique or mechanism of the oppressed who, like himself, were at odds with the robust resolve of the phenomenological world, finding themselves unable to embrace it. In the twilight of his agonizing childhood, he had come up against things whose shapeless existence later dominated him, which he then melancholically accepted for what they were. At the beginning, tears came occasionally, and timidly, whenever evening shadows fell over the courtyards, enveloping the quadrangle in steely blue and rusty brown. Inside, a small garden thrived; between the gooseberry bushes, a meager plum tree grew miserably. The music of the hurdy-gurdy and the harmonica awakened an obsession in him as particles of soot danced in the morning sun, kitchen smells smoldered, and street-side arguments defined the prelude of a life that could only confuse him, and it all seemed to weigh most heavily here at the edge of the city. Isolation, which had checked itself with ingratiating clumsiness, and a sentimentality that he would suppress were the legacies he'd accepted as an omen. And with the violent grip of an incomprehensible power, malicious and sly, the monster that was sex approached him from an obscure realm.

That was the year in which one morning a screaming tore him from sleep, a scream fading away between the walls of neighboring flats then agonizingly repeating itself as if a murderer had broken out of his cell, a scream whose echo alarmed the entire house, followed by quick steps and the slamming of doors. Distressed, still in his nightshirt, he had hurried out of his room.

"Mother, what was that?"

Her embarrassed displeasure brought him back to bed laughing.

"The textile merchant's wife has given birth."

Since that day, an anxiety had overtaken him, an

insidious nagging, a deeply frozen anxiety from within, leading him to be wary of those with a trusting nature, inspiring confidence in forbidden exits, kindling his curiosity in hackneyed fantasies. He scrutinized the bloated bodies of pregnant women lazing about in doorways in the spring, observed their strangely strained facial expressions as blood flowed treacherously through the veins of his neck.

Evil had somehow come suddenly into his world with a brutal, driving force. Already as a small boy, when he folded his hands for his nightly prayers before bed, he was tortured by knowledge of the Devil, He who ruled Hell, deep underground, beyond the land of naïveté. Now, the gates of Hell were unbolted, fire licked at the wood, and the breath of Satan's children came in gasps. Engulfed by disasters, which he sought in vain to understand, he found himself hopelessly adrift, surrounded by an enemy that no one ever called by its name. But its presence was irrefutable and cruel. It made itself known in faltering discussions, ejaculations, and dissolute jokes, in the cracks of doors and within the corners of rooms, where whispering fell silent whenever he interrupted heated conversations with a query. It revealed itself in scraps of newspapers, in shameless scribbles and drawings on walls, a scandalous secret jargon that he observed as if numb. It gave rise to a strange pressure in the pit of his stomach, nervous agitation, a disgusting nausea.

The early years and his first schooldays crawled past, all weighed down with ambivalence, forebodings that extended into the Immeasurable. In the summer, when the July sun oppressively warmed the air in the stairwells, he wasted his vacation on verandas full of ashcans, blew soap bubbles over courtyard gardens, followed swarms of pigeons over the high chimneys with his eyes. Sometimes he was joined by the daughters of the grocer who ran a shop with buttons, soap, salami, and yeast in a tiny alley. They were beautiful, delicate children whom he secretly admired; their copper-colored pigtails and rosy skin gave the impression of a flattering luxury within the poverty of his own surroundings. The younger of the sisters had a particularly ardent way of participating in his games, devising awkward situations with a heroic daring that repelled him and made him unsteady. It seemed he secretly observed the fanatic paleness of her face with feelings from which he would flee.

Between the stairwell and the entrance to the neighboring flat were the doors to the laundry. On afternoons when the sweltering heat under the roof beams foretold rain, he would follow his mother up the rotted wooden stairs and notice there a stubborn and unbearable silence floating amid the boxes of junk in the bluish-red twilight.

The noise from the alley, the music of an organ grinder and the rattle of the wind, remained behind as a whisper barely heard, the muffled echo of a distant din, an almost astonished reverberation. He was enthralled by the secrecy of this hideaway. In his sleep, which drugged him each night like an adventure, seducing him with visions into its landscape, he often saw himself standing in anticipation before the locked stairwell to the roof, waiting decisively with grief and loathing. Sticky with sweat, his hair fell damply onto his forehead; his boyish heart beat with life. When he awoke, set free from the clutches of dream, he nervously sat up in bed, his eyes open wide, and tried to regain his senses. Somewhere, something was scratching and groping; the house's gate creaked and a drunk returned home to his flat on the ground floor. It was on these nights that Blaugast received warning, which at first he resisted in dismay, which fatigued his mind with indifference when it didn't defile it with blind rage.

Once, when his parents were out tending to their affairs in the city center and had left him alone in the summer boredom of the house, he saw the door to the attic standing open. The air, which the day had whisked into a viscous mass, had taken on a pungent luster; a cloud with burning edges darkened the sun as it went past. He climbed the steps and recognized the bright skirt of the grocer's daughter behind the slatted door. Suspicious, with the unfamiliar sensation of committing the forbidden, he pushed himself closer. As he cleared his throat in the half-light, the girl's shriek nearly ripped him apart — he stared wordlessly, dismally becoming aware of his trembling knees.

"What do you want?" she stuttered as his arousal suddenly spread over her.

He only stammered. He turned away, his heavy feet wanting to take him to freedom. He tripped over the laundry basket, yet remained standing, his arms dangling. A minute passed, oppressively, ice cold and boiling hot. Then her hand reached out and pulled him deeper into the alcove. They sat near each other on an overturned washbasin. She was barefoot, her naked legs glowing white in the darkness.

As a young man, whenever Blaugast experienced the seamy, sensuous side of life, moments when he felt released from his self-torment, this afternoon in the attic would always return to him. A whisper crept toward him — the product of a streetwise mind that had furtively carved its confessions into the plaster of the walls. Words darted quickly, a liturgy of evil polluting the tongue. An unholy child's lips hotly sought his mouth; her dress slid up higher; his hands clumsily lost their way.

Temples throbbing, he then tumbled from painful sleep into daylight, which a mounting storm had colored with panicky, shifting shadows. The mystery of the world that troubled him, that studded the miserable heaven of his boyhood with stars like a monstrous, anxious nightmare, had yet to reveal itself. It had become more contradictory, hazier, more wretched. Filth gurgled in the ghostly, vaulted cellars where lepers shuffled lost in the labyrinths, greedily begging for pleasure. Where was the hand that tortured its creatures with flames? And where was love?

Mention was sometimes made of it in books, on scrupulously illustrated pages of well-thumbed pulp novels. Mothers were sitting in polished rooms, their smiles beaming, glowing in feminine grace. Sisters busied themselves peacefully in their rooms, brides waved from balconies decked in flowers. But in their addicted, dilated eyes flickered a fire that consumed the whole world. Under their deceptive garments they had naked, scandalous thighs like the girl in the laundry. Blinded, Blaugast searched for a way out.

That was the intense burden, the legacy he had taken into his own life from the home of his parents. It was forged onto his gait as if a ball and chain — stubborn and clumsy, contemptible, scornful and irrevocable, he couldn't free himself. Whenever he was enjoying the favors of loose women, indulging in the licentious adventures of youth with an ecstasy that had characterized his relationship with the opposite sex from the very beginning, it was nothing more than a pact with the Underworld, infused with a hopelessness that went round in circles, torturing his conscience with anguish. Again and again, whenever whores pounced upon him for a kiss, he felt a desire to meet God. His flesh charred like tinder, the breath of decay came over him, yet he was enraptured by the impulse that yearned for the eternal Spirit.

Once, for a ridiculously short period — two summers and a winter — he had found a clearing in the wilderness. A compassionate woman, who came from somewhere or other, looked after him and, for trivial reasons forever unvoiced, drew closer to him, slowly forcing herself into his silent yoke. Her motherliness enveloped him, and he abandoned himself to it in his hunger for happiness. Just as the world was beginning to illuminate itself, the death that defeated her threw him back into a frenzy that pursued him even into the back room after dull office hours. There, where he lifelessly cursed the grief that plagued him, amid fruitless horror, he lost the strength to go on. There was no longer any will to be found on the path he was pursuing — and then that stormy night lured him outside, and in the glistening glow of the lantern he met Schobotzki, to whom he surrendered his whole being.

III

Morning was already near when Wanda left the whore's dive with her companion. A masked dawn still perched between the houses, and only the edges of the roofs and the outlines of protruding balconies stood in sharp relief against the grayness.

Feeling like an outcast who had lost his way in the fog, Blaugast walked in silence. Incredibly, the day that had been lurking behind sheets of cloud burst forth.

Wanda met his scrutinizing gaze with a laugh.

"Your lover is filthy, my friend. My maid has been away on vacation for a long time. You mustn't look at me."

"You'll take a bath and fix your hair. I'll give you under-wear and clothing. And then you'll be beautiful."

At the threshold of his room, as he turned the key in the lock, a sensation overtook him for a few seconds, as if he were standing before something unspeakable. He'd always had this sense of dread. It would come over him whenever he faced a closed door — a hapless voice that threatened. It had been that way when, as a child, he climbed down the dilapidated steps into the coal cellar, seeking only a crying cat who had lured him to such an heroic undertaking. Thus the row of depraved taverns would greet him, where as a twenty-year-old he had pursued his lewd pleasure. And later, when exhausted by the miasma of the office and yearning for the quiet corner where his companion would welcome him, he would climb the stairs breathlessly — yet the door handle to their flat had an insolent glint that intimidated him with great malice.

When he pressed the switch in the foyer and the white glimmer of the ceiling lamp rose placidly over the stone tiles, the specter retreated. Industriously, he fetched coal and firewood to prepare a crackling fire in the bathroom's oven. Disgust briefly weighed upon him as he took the clothing from the cupboard. Then tenderness again welled inside him; he felt humiliated by its reprimand, and he succumbed to it with much remorse. The days that this chest and its breath represented, the delicacy of life, came back to him, and he realized that they were no longer within his reach, that they had abandoned him.

Wanda took the bundle from his hands without a word of thanks and walked to the bathroom with the air of an old confidante. Blaugast heard the faucet roar; the splashing and the humming went past him like a drowsy commotion after the quiet of the past weeks. A merciless, insipidly piercing daylight exploded behind the curtains. He picked up scattered books, papers, clothing and put them all in the closet, made his bed and sat down near the window. A bit of his feverishness still remained, seeping out of the blanket in which he had wrapped himself; it felt good.

Only now, when a new experience was clearly upon him, and with an absolution that had always secretly displeased him about matters in waking life, did he try to account for his actions, to search for a meaning. The night's encounter stepped imperiously into his consciousness, which the walls of haze and fatigue had temporarily obscured. With a sorrow that only pained and shattered him anew, it became clear to him again what had happened. In his midst was a woman, washing her violated body in his bathroom — a female creature from the realms of unhappiness, animalistic, carefree, and vain.

"Why on earth? — Why?" he asked in ill-humor, searching in vain for a reply.

The face of the dead woman, faded, peered down at him from a fragile frame.

She had not been this way. She was the place of rest that had deceived him, the sweet hoard of bliss blossoming in gold. But now it was here again: the stammering and dread that had dogged him since boyhood on those fatal stairs, the blinded staring at incomprehensible desires, Siberian frosts and tropical dangers. The impudent misery of the words with which his schoolmate had tapped into his confusion now came back to him:

"Are you interested in catastrophes?"

For that one moment of breath, Blaugast became aware of a tiny light colorfully dangling before him, beckoning, a light he had unearthed with both hands from the rubble of his past. Was it not out of charity that he had offered this lost woman a place to stay? Did not kindness tremble with pity when she addressed him in the familiar? Had he, a pilgrim in the mire, not always been on the right trail to the star of mercy?

No. No and no. Between a man and a woman there was no compact possible, no message of dignity. It was the woman's breasts that defeated him, obscene breasts under that discolored cotton calico — visions of hate from the seamy depths where the foul brew of youth seethed. That was the curse tormenting him — that's what made him take her into his house. A last point of pride, burdened with the shabbiness of an inglorious vagrant, resisted self-deception. He recalled the day that the millstone of years had long ago ground to dust, when he had weighed guilt against responsibility, a day resting yellowed and forgotten in the storehouse of eternity. The poison, long boiled away, stirred again in his blood. He had landed with a friend, a painter, in the one-room lodging of a street musician who sometimes rented out his plebian profile by the hour — modeling money. He was not at home, only an old woman crashed about on the floorboards with her wooden leg. Near the stove, her daughter lay in bed bundled in a flannel coverlet, coughing.

"It's her lungs," explained the one-legged woman, as she listened to their instructions. "The doctor believes the creature ought to be stronger, but God will help her, and we are poor people . . ."

The odor of sweat and cooled boiled potatoes made the room inhospitable. The painter threw some change onto the unclean table and turned toward the stairs. Then Blaugast stepped up to the girl's bed. She looked at him with troubled eyes, straightened her covers, but the blanket was worn and not big enough. Under the tatters her leg came into view, baring itself up to the knee. It was an emaciated, sinewy leg that fatally aroused him. In the hollows of its joints, under the curvature of its taut tendons, there were highlights with which he would become familiar.

The painter was impatiently waiting, standing in the doorway with his hat on his head. Blaugast reached into his pocket and laid a banknote in the hands of the sick girl, much too generous for the occasion, much too con-siderable given his financial straits. The consumptive girl thanked him with a greedy expression around her dry mouth. The old woman, frightened, kissed the sleeve of his coat as he followed his friend out into the street, expecting to be chastised for his impropriety.

They parted, and he met the disconcerted reproaches about his magnanimity with an embarrassment of laughter. An acrid taste on his tongue made him nauseous. Blaugast took the words of praise the painter shouted after him as an insult. The feeling of shame that drove him away was caustic, impure. It had always been this way, since the day he could first think. This planet was a storehouse of evil tugging treacherously at its chain. Spies were everywhere. In drafty corners where girls with the precocious faces of children offered flowers and matches for sale, on the oper-ating tables of the clinics, in the miserable suburbs, at train stations, under viaducts: pity was exposed as lust, charity as jealousy. Once he'd been intoxicated by the false splendor of prophecy, which ascetic disciples well-versed in the art of promotion had proclaimed on the market square. Today, only remnants of that feeling were left, problematic shards and fragments that had lingered to scrape his soul like glowing iron filings. Again, for the thousandth time, he placed the question to a godless world: Where was love?

Freezing, Blaugast sank into his armchair. The weight of a great, hollow loneliness oppressed him. He looked around the room as the early morning drearily undressed the wall. A tearless sobbing burst his breast, bent him forward to grasp the emptiness with his arms that he fell face first onto the carpet. Having led his life upstairs and down in obscene diversions that tested the limits of his manhood, the irreversible that was now upon him trampled his body, defiled his humanity. From the days of his youth, far from this desolate torture, a friendship sometimes remained with him, an earnestness that gripped serenely for his hand, a camaraderie that trusted; it was always the one thing that artfully loosened the latticed bars of paradise to let the golden bird of loyalty quickly fly around the corner. There was a person who had matched his heart with his own, and who, like a brother, had revealed himself on late-night walks through the city. But the red tip of a woman's tongue had proved stronger than this alliance. Between clusters of stones, growing out of barren piles of sand — destroyed years and difficult times — Blaugast saw the flower of passion. A burning obsession raised its head, perhaps for the last time. His hand was numb and no longer opened. The hopelessness of his torment so stuck in his throat that, without knowing why, he madly bit into the weave of the carpet and groaned.

A noise made him pause. Wanda had finished her bath and now stood in front of him, freshened, in a fluffy housecoat, with a look of reproach:

"Are you drunk?"

Her black hair, combed and parted, was wet. A displeased fold pressed her eyebrows together as she held out her stout foot, now shod in a slipper.

"Tie my slippers tighter. And be sensible." Blaugast raised himself wearily to his knees. A searing pain shot through his shoulders and back as he fastened the leather thong over her skin. Sighing, his mouth bowed lower and lower, until his forehead touched her radiant leg, until his lips abandoned themselves to a kiss — a branding.

Wanda gazed in silence at the stooped figure.

"Stand up!" she commanded, almost whispering.

And as he swayed, bleary-eyed under the invisible burden, she let her robe glide to the ground. Tall, plump and naked, she stood before him. Under her eyelashes he caught sight of her pupils, dilated and dull. Her vulgar breasts heaved lustfully as he spread out his arms to her with a cry of agony; then he sank down in a blaze.

A torrent swept away the pangs of conscience, lust, and loathing.

Fate had come to Blaugast out of the tunnels of night. An apocalyptic woman had seized him. As if a storm had brought with it a raging din, funeral music, blood from the depths. Like a lifeless stone, he sank to the bottom, into the throes of sex, into the insanity of his fate, into the sleep of the damned.

IV

Whatever ecstatic pleasure Blaugast had experienced with women always left him disappointed. The transparency of vulgar anticipation and the discharge of passionate revolts went limp in his realm, never achieving instinctive sexual force, never taming the turmoil to which he felt himself subjugated. The feeble heroic deed of forming a union to find pleasure in the sating of urges was suspect and lowly to him, a work of illusion he rejected in disbelief. Over the course of years he had killed with hope, when, true to his nature, he went chasing after new promises again and again, the peculiar would brush up against him, the unusual caress him — and frailty was driven further into the corner.

An aura surrounded him, conjuring traces of feminine desire and surreptitiously luring the girls of his drinking buddies into his embrace. Something anxious, seeking help, something blind and vague armed with wrath against the modesty of banal experience, met depravity halfway, cooled passion with ice. He was not comfortable with the bourgeois rapture of cheap actresses in search of memories lifted from a book. The frozen passion of these encounters wasn't worth the deceit, for which he had to pay.

There was one with a glassy face, worn-out from cruel trickery, a plain hairdo, and sleep-deprived eyes that glimmered under the brow of her tortured mask. She was the bride of a brilliant, crazy student who eagerly poached in the outlying hedges of science; Blaugast spent the hours of night with him in miserable bars. Sometimes they would take an outing as a threesome, listen to a brass band in the dusty cool of a suburban garden, or enter, either cheerfully or dejected, into the trappings of endless conversations in the gloomy shack of a Dalmatian winebar. The girl, as amicable as a man without revealing the ultimate nature of her gender, of which she was keenly aware, gladly took his side when there arose differences of opinion. She was a language teacher, new to the city, and had time to spare for short trips at the end of the day.

On one holiday morning beyond the city's outskirts, while her boyfriend drowned the nightmare of an unyielding storm in the water of a meek current, the two of them remained behind together, guarding the man's clothes hidden in the reeds. Blaugast took her hand, which was caressing a sun-charred wildflower. His kiss, seeking as it explored, dug into her skin above the wrist; she withstood it without protest.

At lunch in the overgrown arbor of a riverside inn, her fingers spread to stroke the discolored mark.

"What happened to you?" asked the student.

Absentmindedly, like a playful child, she glanced at the obvious spot.

"It was an ant!" she declared, smiling. Then she got tired and pressed for a return home.

The following day Blaugast received a letter in a handwriting unfamiliar to him.

"That was no ant, my love. On the riverbank, between the thistles and the lizards' lairs, a beautiful man sweetly wounded me on the hand . . ."

It was the prelude to a futile love, firmly rooted in the undergrowth of false abandon. After midnight, when her fiancé had gone to bed, she would once again leave the house to meet with Blaugast in front of the entrance to a remote, silent hospital, or in parks, where they shamefully and hurriedly fell into one another's arms in the darkness of night. The crow of the rooster in a faraway dell drew these trysts to a close. There were also hours where she met him secretly in the room she had lived in as a young single woman, in the loveless prison of a wretched governess's existence, where suitcases draped in rugs made pretense to an obstinate divan, where simple household amenities and bare surroundings gave rise only to condemnation, self-reproach, and hysteria. The distress of her loneliness that tottered between the two men inspired her to a peculiar thought. Terrified by the symbolism that in the wells of her being administered the worship of her femininity according to an unclear hierarchy, she divided her body into two halves and gave to one that which she denied the other. Her waist was the limit to which she would tolerate advances and which, in this way, protected her from a seduction whose goal it was to possess her entirely. Her instinctive nature was defended by a stratagem of war that had sprung from a desire for vindication and was intended to enable her, in a most clever way, to be loyal to two lovers at the same time. Blaugast grew despondent from the tiresome whims of this foolishness.

Then there was the innkeeper's daughter, the girl who occupied his thoughts over the years and initiated his first breakdown. As a seventeen-year-old, escaping the confines of the ramshackle business that was her ancestral inn, the patient serving of customers, she was languidly and awkwardly caught in a double bind — professional haggling and procurement had offered her a home. When Blaugast picked her up, a joint-stock company of sorts, a circle of rakish youths especially fond of her type, had established itself around her. They were a half-dozen carefree connoisseurs who had pooled their spare change to jointly share the costs of her love's delights. The narrow corridor room of an eager widow, food and service included, was an extravagance, but one that had been adequately adjusted in respect to the salaries of these willing assistants, athletic trainers, and bank trainees. Small gifts from this or that hand, lingerie and silk scarves of an especially obligated generosity, lent a personal touch to the enterprise. Blaugast knew of this resourceful group of entrepreneurial youths only from hearsay. He was the cuckoo interloping in another's nest without being required to pay for expenses and their compounded interest. And yet, every so often he got a taste of the collapse of this cooperative's principles, the faults in its mechanism.

Following an afternoon excursion through meadows and forests, drinking coffee in a village garden and in the evening exhausted by the sun and fresh air, they would fall victim to their love, which hurried their trip home. Climbing the stairs with one another, excited and passionate, exchanging in the hall reckless kisses that painfully heightened his urgency, it often happened that he would abruptly leave the oppressiveness of the room because the tobacco haze and carelessly scattered clothes were signs of the presence of their owner, who was waiting complacently in bed for her return. Blaugast always came home after the prosaic conclusion of such adventures with the bitter taste of an undeservedly ugly humiliation.

Or there was the bizarre relationship, inhibited by superstitious practices, with the depraved salesgirl, who was regarded by ranks of experts as a genius of unleashed eroticism. The maze of her pleasures was bordered by commemorative days, reserves of chastity into which she would unexpectedly flee. On the night her mother died, or on the wedding day of her parents, the oil flame burned under the blackened icon reverently inherited from a pious childhood. Such a date was undeniably tied to an abstinence that managed to celebrate lovers' trysts with introspection, and to conversations that lay far from the practice and goal of contritely interrupted embraces.

Thus were the episodes that filled the trashbins of a thoughtlessly squandered youth. The aimless loathing of these events, cloying in their pursuit of him, fertilized a resignation that vied with yearning. Despite this, he wasn't strong enough to turn his back in disgust on the musty designs of these matters. Somehow, he was tied to the circumstances of the salesgirl's emotions, her stale scent; somehow, it compelled him to encourage her in the superficial wonder of her deceit, to keep climbing the ladder that never led out — out of vacant coffeehouses or the casemates of brothels. That is, until a small, zealously buried scar fermented in his brain an essence that clouded in froth the translucent image of his inner visions.

It was in the cheap, poorly ventilated, tawdry parlor of a seedy winebar that the incomprehensible gripped him. To be sure, after a night of carousing, done with the aimless joy of the indifferent, an uneasiness would often signal a warning to him: as if he were a mountaineer standing on the edge of an abyss, suddenly overwhelmed by horror. In such moments, his vision of the world, reduced to irony, removed itself to a distance that evaded the grip of his hands. The humming of invisible insect wings struck a chord in him, unbearable murmuring from the catacombs, the anxious difficulty of breath in the enormous well of the Banished. This time, he found himself prostrate on a patch of floor covered in spit experiencing the terror of being suddenly abandoned by reliable instincts, of spiraling out of control. A clamor, screams for help and steps droned in his head. He heard the bony rattling of his teeth in his mouth, how his loosened jawbones disobediently mangled the Lord's Prayer.

The clinic's assistant doctor, whom he sought out the next morning, read the history of his sickness from the reflex of his pupils. Politely, with dry wording, he gave him an unembellished diagnosis and went on to attack the malady with an injection. Blaugast pressed his lips together when he comprehended the verdict. Everything out of his mildewed past that had inexorably clustered into reality was now confirmed, irrefutably proven. And the ire of the swindled, of one who has paid a premium for an item that spinelessly slips from his grasp, now played a wicked, mean trick and descended on him like a slimy cloud, oppressive, depriving him of future prospects.

After years of idle waiting and repulsion, the death of his ladylove brought about the second crisis. A mortal pain, disgusting beyond measure, lay for a short while in his loins, boring into his muscles entire nights like a thick syringe. Shameful daydreams came, wild crimes of an inflamed fantasy that worked their treachery and eclipsed his consciousness. Whenever he came back to himself out of the tortuously long stretches of these illusions, the wickedness of his carcass swelled like a monster in the room to extinguish the lamp at his bedside.

Weeks passed before he was able to find his way out of these meanderings in this hellish hall of mirrors — the stupor of one maimed by an explosion, the apathy of a cripple — back into the vicious cycle, the same route circled again and again: office duty and coincidences, nighttime sleep and the need to eat. Yet during breaks from his mindless work, havoc began to gather within him. The asceticism that had been forced upon him escaped through leaky holes. The restlessness of his blood scraped against the prison ramparts, sticking shadows and scenes there as if magically projected. It scratched tirelessly at his mind, pulsated fiercely in his temples. It came swarming out of the trenches and blinds from all directions. Faces with open mouths, women up for sale, offering their finest, the unhappy death rattle. Blaugast was well acquainted with this fervor, which was more like frost, a lukewarm hoar, barren fields. Whenever he sank into his bed at home, overcome by obstacles he was too exhausted to recognize, his heart stomped in time, chugging like the pistons of a machine. Thus went this journey by rail, its unavoidable tracks leading past eerie slopes and fainthearted stations into the Unknown.

V

With Wanda, though, it was different. The wishful think-ing of his youth, his body's secret, seemed to find fulfillment in her. Health and abundant energy were found in her store, the infallible defense of a simple creature who combats the rebellions of the flesh with a casual ease. It was the unbro-ken strength of a peasant ancestry that could handle such foolhardiness, arrogantly managing any complication. The uninhibited calm with which she had looked after her parent's livestock as an adolescent also served her well in dealing with men.

The Bohemian landscape that embraced her woman-hood had little to do with obstacles and difficulties. There was the farm with the stalls where cows leisurely digested the steaming feed, the village road, and the pigsty. There was the goose pond, its gloomy surface sometimes rippled by the wind that brightly, and without emotion, passed over the flat hollow to rest itself on the edge of the high plain, amid the ruddy fields of grain. There were the crudely assembled sections of wall, made of dung and angular stone, moldy hedges, wild pepper, and white-gold chamomile. There was the sap of the cherry trees, dripping slowly in small drops out of cracked bark, melting in your mouth, freely, with a taste of summer, the rough texture of the organic. Everything that grew there was governed by laws accepted without question, was naturally bound to the earth: the weeds between the stiff stalks of wheat, rainstorms and harvest; strokes of a cane for working too slowly, the reek of animals, the sweat of workers. There, simple obedience in the face of life was to be found in one's blood, ripened in the sun. Her sleep was heavy, able to carry an immense load, a huge clod of earth — an expanse behind the village amidst the fields. The good, the bad, the uncontrollable and evil crept through the pores of her body without feeling obliged to change state. This persisted even when she went to work in the city, to land in the harbor of prostitution with eyes open, as strong as ever, and with the mocking attitude of those "in the know."

In Blaugast's case, it had taken her, with the instinct of a divining rod, only a short time to discover his inconstant melancholy, the fundament of his existence. The stormy night that blew them together held its breath only now and again, never entirely flagging. Its tumult, its dangerous threat, echoed in apprehensive pauses, deathly-silent, as the tunnel of his obsession opened itself up to light; the morning spat out its day's work when Wanda's blunt chin rose from the hollow of the neighboring pillow. It had just happened that she'd stayed, and it never occurred to him, even in passing, to hint at curtailing the company she had forced upon him. His sick leave, which had freed him from the office during the weeks of merciless decay, was now at an end; he didn't possess enough savvy to take any steps to extend it.

The figures he had had to laboriously calculate, the balance of accounts recorded in Faustian-like ledgers, had left his network of nerves in peculiar agitation. A leak had sprung in his vessels, clotted together in the chaos of ill-disposed urges, through which turbid sewage seeped as if escaping a metal hull. The gloominess of his surroundings — frayed scraps of paper, toilet odor, his blotter — produced a scandalous contrast, outrageous, kicking maliciously in the snarl — all because he had relied upon illusions squandered in futility.

There had been a time when, in the colorfully-glazed days of reading random novels, he had willingly granted admission to all those dreams, idiosyncratically ornate, that redeemed him from the stuffy air of reality, thrusting him into the abundance of unknown lands. The sea and the continents, the supple accent of southern dialects, adventurous voyages and Homeric landscapes — all were embodiments that tempted brightly and resonated broadly with his imaginings. The faces of Spain, Italian beggar children, Tyrolean mountains with the ringing of cowbells and country churches — all appeared in his realm, only to fly off hopelessly, in vain. Then there were the women, products of an unfortunate brooding, who stepped into their place. Distant travels, tremendous experiences with women — these were the pursuits that nagged him. Blaugast recognized angrily, with undignified disgust, that both had remained denied to him. On city squares or park promenades, whenever he met a lady whose profile attracted him, whose sleekly-formed legs made his heart skip a beat, he felt her slipping away — her brief reprimanding glance, her haste to a trivial destination, a vague insult. He took it as a personal affront and it enraged his sense of justice when in the tram, opposite him, just one step away, the tall female passengers of his dreams took their seats without his having the right to speak with them, to assign them the tasks appropriate to all the wild possibilities of his meticulous fantasies. Namely, it was those whose beauty already bore that gracefully blurred character of maturity that he looked upon with pain, revolting against the absurdity of a world that withheld what was due his impassioned soul. Harbingers of autumn, whose well-kept skin resembled the fruits of late harvest, affected him the most strongly. Blaugast gritted his teeth when, after experiencing an embarrassed strangeness, he secretly sensed a woman's private self and the briefly-known passenger would get off at the next stop.

From the very beginning, Wanda had spied the trapdoor that sealed the storeroom of his repressions. She had cunningly recognized that the hunger wearing on him wasn't one to be fed a nourishing fare, the midday meal of diners indifferent to the exquisiteness of the cuisine. Indeed, she knew that his yearning stemmed from sources shrouded in the mystical, that devotion and fulfillment had to be inventive in their variations in order to dazzle this unfortunate being, to moor such a nomadic soul. She sensed that it wasn't anything particular, but Woman in her entirety, the Platonic archetype of Creation, toward which he strove. Motherliness, the irrefutable legacy of a ponderous peasant lineage, the criminal innocence of her limitations, only gave her the upper hand, which she was used to having anyway — all to offer the customers of her trade as expressions of her heretically abandoned femininity. Without fail, it was always the most gullible whom she took in.

Blaugast found his way, obediently, into the depraved hotbeds of her willing sexuality. The spare change of her artful ecstasies seemed like profligate riches to his impoverished soul. Culture, far removed from her coarsely-trained senses, was replaced by experience. He understood, and was thankful, that she didn't treat the wandering nature of his virility as a simple trifle, as had perhaps occurred earlier, when he'd insisted on clearing uneven ground like a skilled gardener, or to poach sentimentally in virgin forests.

Wanda knew to steer through his sensitive attentions like a blind passenger and had the courage to stay the course through his moods like a ship at sea, not attempting to pull his caprice out of tune, always remaining completely in the picture. Her brilliance was to grasp quickly; her adaptability approached the very limits of excess. When she once noticed in passing how he glanced at the exposed knee of a schoolgirl, she fashioned herself a risqué costume while he brooded listlessly at the office; dressed in a school uniform with generously shortened knee stockings, she waited for his arrival home.

She tackled the peripheral regions of his depression, those thoughts that overcast his alert sex, with all manner of obstructions and tricks, which, brazenly invented, weighed down on him and oppressed. From the courtesans of chivalrous times, when in a mistress's boudoir the dignity of the king became transformed into servility, she had adopted the heroic role, and so yoked the wiles of women past to her festive, triumphal cart. To ensure her total control, she loaned out her assets when it seemed appropriate, relinquished a web of jealousy only suited for downgrading the value of the sacrificial beast. Like a slave owner who observes with pleasure the progress and health of her charges, who avoids ill-treatment so as not to injure precious flesh, she always took care to gorge the demands of her partner with promises. Not content to allow his restlessness the complete freedom which he required in affairs of the heart, she sought occasions to spark the engine of passion, to share the windfalls of his pleasure as an observer. Her relation to the demimonde and adjacent terrain was like a worm-rotted footbridge that Blaugast, encouraged by her approval, ambitiously crossed to exceed any past achievements, conquests now regarded only with cynicism.

The zeal with which Wanda seized hold of the control mechanism she found in the deadlock of his addictions was itself a dark danger, inundating him with ambiguity. She took control of his pedantic mind, of his violently confused and desperate urges, then drew up a manifest of his corrupted ideas, thereby vanquishing the hindrances of humiliated pride. She brought him coquettes well-versed in the methods of coy rejection, also vigorous society ladies who still retained a shred of respectability in the frenzy of their nocturnal industry, wasting their blushes between supply and demand.

She carefully collected whatever had come to naught in the course of his forays and lonely years, presenting them expertly bundled as if a bouquet. His blood, pathologically cool, was set in motion through bald lies. Spurious histories of misbegotten urges, false resistance that could be bought, blackmailing vice — all whirled into his house as if a warning staged by Wanda.

In her circle of friends, who derived uncertain pleasure from this newfound entertainment, experiments were discussed in order to test the threshold of Blaugast's temperament within given roles. Gentle reflections came into the unpleasant light of amateurish coincidences, then cruelly dissipated into mere filth. He suddenly found himself in the middle of an enterprise to which he had yielded without thought, which washed up strange debris in the murk of his imaginary world. This curious swarm of sprites passed on the news of his endeavors in whispers. Once given free rein, this gossip was never allowed to rest. Pagegirls, attired in boys' jackets and tight velvet pants, served meals that soon degenerated into orgies, but only after the proper pedantic ceremony. The spark of puberty smoldered in the faces of debauched children, wanton kisses kindled the memory of bridal anxieties. It was war, and Blaugast quartered this force in his silent, hostile castle. The female servants looked on palely, the mistress of the house came with her daughter to greet the officer whose property they'd all recently become. Garments rustled, affected speech humbled itself into stammering. On the Island Kingdom of the Damned, where he fished for gold ingots, he brought long-buried oaths to light, which again attained purity in sophisticated embraces. Dormant idylls woke him from suffocation. Lesbians offered their dilatory rapture for sale. The cheap booze Wanda plied him with destroyed his will, his upright composure, his supreme sense of integrity. Addiction drew its paws around him and the vulgar bourgeois existence.

VI

Of those observing the unholy acts conjured up by Wanda according to one of her many scenarios — none of which she ever conceived in advance — Johanna was the least corrupted. The alleyway that meant professional obligation for her, that her mature reason nimbly accepted, the clattering of high heels on cobblestones moistened by dew, the sweet burn of the cheap, slimy liquor in bars — none had destroyed her natural country sensibilities. Something in her was in conflict with the impertinence of her desires, with the filth of these depraved scraps; nonetheless, degeneracy still had the upper hand. Her voice had completely turned in on itself; she limped unattractively and mischievously into a hateful falsetto. But in rare moments a small cracked bell rang inside her, a plea for alms.

She had gotten to know Blaugast while playing a part in a love scene that Wanda had staged in his flat as a homage to him. The joyless trumpery, the presumptuousness of these living dreams behind which the ludicrous flickering of a guttering candle beamed as stage lighting, inspired in her a sense of pity and precocious arrogance.

As the group departed and the host lingered limp, withering on the ottoman, a furious address made his head jump from the pillow.

"Why are you doing this? — It isn't worthy of you!"

The words hit Blaugast like a vulgar cliché — the heroic truth of humanistic concepts brought in from afar, glistening into the desperate disorder of his dwelling, where the air hung sluggish with the smell of nude female bodies. — It wasn't worthy of him. Where had he heard such a superhuman expression before? The old grammar book bound in cracked canvas leafed disturbingly through his thoughts. Wasn't it that time when he and Schobotzki were together, far beyond in the realm of legions and Roman armor? Greedy, knowledgeable, mindful, blessed, imperious and fulfilled — he saw Johanna standing before him in her slutty street clothes as he looked stunned into her bold expression. How did this whore from Wanda's stable come to have such eyes?

Heartburn scratched at his throat, his answer was hoarse.

"Not worthy of me? This undoubtedly appears to be correct. But I am a dog, Johanna, and I do have to howl."

It took him by surprise when an excessive force, a train hurled over the embankment by Divine Providence, pressed down on him like a great weight. Something that appeared to be steadfast, shreds of remaining pride, shored up by dilapidated blocks, was blasted away by the chill — wore away, turned to dust. He sprang to his feet, staggered imploringly, the caricature of a Defender, the tree on a cliff bracing itself against landslide. The thought of flight pulled him back down to earth. He stuffed his handkerchief down his throat. But it was too late. Huge and disgraceful, bawling burst from within him. He bellowed malevolently, like an animal, but instead of running away a great torrent gushed out.

At that moment, Wanda, shrouded in hostility, stormed out of the kitchen. Her skirt, hastily buttoned, slopped about like a compress on her legs, a light blue bra stretched taut and indecent under her shirt. The twig she had roasted over the gas to blacken her eyebrows was stuck like a dagger between clenched fingers. She squinted distrustfully at Johanna, who timidly accepted such scrutiny with dismay.

"What's the fool doing? Does he want to get us turned in to the police, or does he want to be put in a straitjacket?"

Angrily, she kicked the trembling man, and Blaugast rolled himself away from her like an insensate lump. His mouth, exhausted and distorted, gasped for insults, craving filth and horror.

"You degenerate — get away from me — don't touch me, you whore —"

Wanda gazed for a moment at his wretched form. At odds with the situation, mockery pursed her lips.

"Wimp!" she hissed back in contempt. Then she turned on her heel and slammed the door.

Caught up in the impropriety, Johanna made a move to follow. Then she suddenly took control of herself and stood meager and dark in the corner.

"Are you angry with me, Mr. Blaugast?"

It was the question of a child who had caused a disruption and was sorry for it.

Blaugast shook himself, with distraught hands swept the hair from his forehead, raised himself and stumbled. He fell onto the chair that Johanna had brought him, grabbed for her dress, choking on what was unsaid.

"Oh no, oh no. What would make me do that? Who am I then, a man among men, a tiny, wretched Klaudius? — But you have to understand me, Johanna — you mustn't leave without understanding that!"

"I'll try. But you have to calm down."

"Love is customer service, a picture book or panorama. Peepholes are cut into its lining, then a sudden jerk, and the box grows bright again. Marked are those who have seen something different than their neighbors. There are those who are wise, though wounded and orphaned. You belong to them, too, but you just don't see it, Johanna."

"You're ill, Mr. Blaugast. I'm almost frightened of you —"

"We're all ill. The light's ill, the wick of the lamp, the darkness and the anxiety as well. There's a nerve leading from the mind to the loins. A beautiful nerve, artful in its arrangement, nourished by little vessels that rush to and fro. A favorite of our dear, loving Lord and His Providence. There one can conjure up gentle clouds, bleating lambs on the village green, and flowering meadows. Unseen, however, the thread has unwound itself, has become shredded, a fraying tightrope over a glacier. Suddenly, everything is transformed. The lambs have vanished, the moonlight has crept away, crocodiles lie in wait in the marshy banks —"

"Why do you tell such stories?"

"Because you are a woman, Johanna, and women are the secret. You cannot open it and you cannot reveal it. You have no knowledge of it. — You *yourself* are it. But I am condemned night and day, all the hours and years of my life to chase after it. And it's difficult for me, more difficult than you suspect. Everything is good, well conceived, sweet and pleasant. The sky is bright blue, flocks of lambs are rosy red, bellflowers ring in the field. But there is that cord, the tightrope over the abyss slowly cut by the edge of the stone. I can no longer differentiate the real from the supernatural. I have images of women in my head, revealing something that attacks and plunders like a forest bandit. I can't see it clearly. It's contorted, hidden, as if cubist. The woman being dressed for her wedding, the lady in a riding costume, the gracious madam, the princess. Promises are to be found in the groans of ecstasy, which exist somewhere, and yet I can't find them. It's awful, my dear Johanna, to be alone with these things. No one was there, no one wanted to help me —"

"And you believe that's what Wanda has in store for you? —"

"Yes, you see, Wanda — she understands the ways of the world, what I can be caught with, and what can bring me down. But catharsis is lacking, the fulfillment of the purification. She fed me sugar when I was hungry for bread. She began a six-day siege when, in the struggle with sexuality, I was assailing the very dignity of which you've reminded me. I'm the man who goes overboard in the middle of the ocean and cannot swim. I'm afflicted with a plague, only to experience the moment that sets me free and dissolves me, the moment I have pursued since childhood. It's for that reason I need a woman. I foresee the curves of her figure, which always disperse as soon as I open my eyes. Whenever a woman swings her hem in passing, breathes behind me in the theater, I feel a part of her. It's never the entirety. Never the skin upon which my fluids dissipate. I have no time to wait and be still. I'm surrounded by names and shapes that constantly confuse me. There's the woman who sobs when kissing, the woman in the velvet dress, the woman with the exposed knees. Everything is different inside me, hotter and more unbearable. I'm talking nonsense, I know that. That's the scary thing, that no sense comes of it. Bawling behind the veiled doors of smutty desires, I'm the man overboard, that's it, Johanna. I'm the drowning man clinging to straw."

Johanna didn't reply. A man was in agony, a mountain spewing out lava and ash.

"How is it with others? — I don't dare judge it. There is evil inside me, sensuously zigzagging along that nerve and always the same path, from the brain to the groin. Everything else is blocked, buried by pure chance, eaten full of holes by termites. I sit in the office and study files. An ink spot on the blotter seems to me extremely suggestive. An unconscious woman stands wedged between the letters. There is a bench in the park. A wicked knife has carved some obscenity into the wood. There is a church, and I want to pray. The high altar is perfumed with incense, a harem window, colorful and gilded. Do I know, do you know, what the angels indulge in behind those bars? He who loves abundantly will be greatly forgiven. And I gaze transfigured under the skirts of the Mother of God."

Blaugast sat collapsed in his armchair. His chin slid down his chest; his body lacked definition, like that of a young boy's. Johanna squatted down, snuggled like a child to the side of the sunken figure. Her voice was gentle, timid yet imploring. She spoke of the time when she, the baby of the family, fell asleep in the lap of their old servant, when she once fed the seagulls flying over the Moldau while boarding at the home of a stranger. The simple glimmer of irretrievable happiness that had brightened the first half of her youth darted through the room. Disheveled dolls with rosy cheeks, the sound of the music box she had received one Christmas. That was a melody she had never forgotten, even as the tavern music gnawed at her past. A cheerful mood rang throughout, a time of pure innocence, the ambiance of a fairy tale.

Johanna quietly sang, and the song spread its wings, silhouetting the two of them.

Then came the hard times when she was living at home again, after her loving mother took ill and she, a twelve-year-old girl, had to sell shoelaces door-to-door. "What is hunger?" she had earlier thought as she picked at the sugared beans on her plate during more prosperous times. She asked that question no more. And so it went, as it always goes, whenever a thin young girl in a torn dress runs about in the street, climbs decrepit stairs, patiently rings doorbells, knocks at the doors of bachelors to ask if they need new shoelaces. When the woman, dead-tired, broken and alone, was picked up by the corpsman, Johanna was brought to a house in which jewelry and clothes were abundant, bowls of candy, sweet-talking foolishness. No longer a beggar child, she was a young woman.

"Miss Johanna," — whispered the madam. "You're the finest of them all."

Was it not a stroke of luck, a resurrection, a home-coming?

Johanna continued with her story. The elegance of the massage parlor glowed in her words, overwhelmed her. That happens only once in a lifetime, it doesn't come around again. There was chatting, cajoling and mockery, card games and all things social. Once in a vanishing dream, when the music box chirruped, she had always been alone. Suddenly she had sisters. Suddenly there was a bed, luxurious and softly cushioned; there were wasted mornings, a mirror on the wall, powder-puffs and happiness. She wasn't able to remember what happened to her later. The years soon brought filth, winter worries, commotion. One can't always stay at home. It's already too much to have been there once. Everyone has to work, each in their own way.

Blaugast remained motionless. She also quieted, overcome in an embarrassed silence, and sat. Her lifeless face, robbed of its beauty by the trade, was near his. As if siblings, in the dying intermission that followed his outburst, her words of comfort had come to his aid.

"It's fine, Johanna," he said in passing. "Now go home!"

As they shook hands like shy schoolchildren, each heart woven into the other's, the coming dusk lost its terror. Without knowing it, they had made a pact with one another — the outlaw and the woman who sold the reflection of an acquired smile to the man-beast around the corner for the sum of fifty crowns.

VII

The conversation with Johanna, when he had hysterically broken down upon realizing the wretchedness of his failure, marked a change in the relationship between Blaugast and Wanda. The care with which she'd cultivated their little garden of heavenly desire, the opportunities in the realm of his pleasures, had turned to rejection, to an indifferent obstinacy, a withered existence. Vexed by enmity and his nightly orgies, he had given up his job at the office, which until now had afforded him security, for a severance pay that would not satisfy his spendthrift ways for long. Now, he loafed about idly at home, slept until noon, turning his head toward the wall in exhaustion whenever the demands of the increasingly insufferable deliverymen and the annoyance of bills due roused him from bed.

Wanda reacted against the transformed situation in her own way, being in possession of stringent recipes for his weak passivity. At the beginning, she tended to his apathy

— which allowed adverse circumstances to encroach without his resistance — with undisguised contempt. Anger over the uncertainty of a sanctuary she was determined not to surrender, disappointment over the inglorious collapse of her financial security — all this allowed her to forget the nature of their elective friendship. She made no attempt to rouse him from his lethargy, to shore up his will to live, to give him purpose. As unexpected as it was unequivocal, she refused him the tribute that was the justification of their union. Her body, which still excited him, was no longer in his possession. Unconcerned with the problematic nature of the physical that left him so shattered, she stubbornly rejected him until he became a useless wanderer among the clutter of her household goods, a parasite whom she punished with displeasure. The female companions of her trade, whom she had previously set on the humble solicitor, stayed away in fright since the rumor of his breakdown had made the rounds of the quarter. With malicious intent, threatening and merciless, she kept watch over his doorstep. Even Johanna, who put on the child-like smile reserved only for acts of mercy and visits to the infirmed, had to retreat in humiliation when Wanda, without word of explanation, locked the bolt in her face. Instead, though only occasionally at first, and then with increasing frequency, the men started to come — the clientele from Wanda's infamous practice, men who visited her in her room, paying for their great pleasure with money from which her worthless room-mate got a pittance as alms on the more profitable days.

With a mysterious paralysis, Blaugast felt the drastic change to which his condition was headed. The suffering that had him under its control, tormenting him with vile pains, had hollowed him out, wrested away the strength needed to defend himself. Monstrously, like the wolf in the children's fable, horror raised its head when stifled whispers, a sensuous secret, took shape for the first time in the room next door — to ruin him. Limp and exhausted, numbed by sedatives, hair unkempt, he had appeared then in the doorway of the room, gaudily cheapened by the effusive scent of eau de Cologne, makeup, folded paper flowers, and a rust-red lampshade. A thickset young man with a patched tie arrayed loosely under his shirt collar was standing there with legs apart, buttoning up his suspenders.

Wanda sat backward on a chair in front of the vanity and powdered her breasts. She didn't look up when he leaned against the lintel, panting and corpse-like, unshaven, eyelids swollen and shirt open. Only her upper teeth gnawed on her lower lip as his dumbfounded gaze wandered over the scene, meeting her domineering expression in the mirror.

"Who is that?" asked the man, smoothing a crumpled

handkerchief with his thumbs and blowing his nose noisily.

"That's my landlord. He serves me," answered Wanda without turning around. "He'll fetch warm water for us from the kitchen —"

As Blaugast remained standing with sunken shoulders, his spine giving way, ingenuous, incapable of comprehending, she began yelling loudly and stuck out her saliva-soaked tongue.

"Didn't you hear me, idiot? — You're supposed to bring water for me and the gentleman —"

Blaugast nodded. Something nasty and pale was rising up gigantically before him; like a dust cloud before a thunderstorm it approached, darkening his consciousness. He finally understood. Tired, legs buckling, he shuffled into the kitchen. He filled the vessels from the pot on the oven as if an obedient machine driven by mechanical forces. Washwater, stale and tepid, trickled disgustingly over his fingers. He took no notice. Clumsy and wooden, feeling as if his body were set with hinges, he carried the pot and the bowl back to the room.

That was the beginning. It was a confusion that unreasonably and perniciously took over his service, entering the scene ostentatiously with cigar ash and cheap whiskey, nighttime visits and laundry stained with sweat. Rudderless, a ship dead in the water, he did the work as he was ordered. The coins it earned, a paltry exchange of thanks from satisfied lodgers, those who needed a helping hand after a full night of love-making, felt greasy. Their ringing, shameful clatter was exchanged for cigarettes that he greedily smoked, for golden cognac that burned like an unquenchable disgrace in his mouth, without which he couldn't go on.

Wanda understood her business. She knew the scum of the lower class who, without any talent, were familiar with the depths: where explosive gases glowed beyond support beams, and miners' lanterns lit up the path downward, disappearing underground. Merchants came, to whom a successful trade brought in the bacon that fattened them up, asthmatic waiters and shabby intellectuals, who had no difficulty in conforming in bed to the manners of their milieu. Blaugast took the orders of his benefactors as a matter of course. With a brush he scrubbed the street's dried excrement from clothes unabashedly cast off. He made cocoa for Wanda, fetched beer from the neighboring inn. He was set up with matches that he handed discreetly through the crack in the door to patrons impatient and overbearing, and brought in freshly ironed handkerchiefs for the more fastidious. A pathological squinting accelerated by alcoholism had suddenly disfigured his face, making it restless and ridiculous. Awareness of what had gathered around him went astray. He slept, drank from the bottle that stood near the lamp, quickly flew into his slippers whenever Wanda called or a guest requested him. Under his skin, ravaged by innumerable stings as if from armies of ants, he often had the feeling that his body was flagging. Memories of earlier times, the struggle for God and purpose, were gone. He no longer knew what happened in the world. It was enough that he had tobacco and his daily cognac. He was the golem, bewitched by incantation, unquestioningly performing his duty.

One morning, after an anxious night's sleep, strangeness burrowed from behind the wall and into his ear. A rip in the pit of his heart, an invisible wound incessantly, senselessly rent by a knife sopping with salt and vinegar, threw him from bed and set him on his feet, staggering. He gathered his wits. A customer had arrived late at night whom Wanda had to let in herself, as he had been gripped by a fit of coughing. The curses she had used to subdue his nervous, uncontrollable sobbing had been ineffective. Now it was time to prepare breakfast. The restlessness next door signaled departure.

The dividing door opened imperiously, two men's boots, crusty from the rain of the previous day, clapped down before his feet.

"Clean these shoes, Klaudius!" sounded the command. Wanda's voice was dry and surly, hostile and dangerous.

Blaugast took up the tin can and the rag. For the first time, he noticed that his hands had become initiated into deformity, how the paralysis of his spine, which was causing him to misstep, had hindered, too, the grip of his fingers. Between the askew eyelets, the shabby remains of a tongue hung out — the leather, chewed up by moisture, stretched itself out shamelessly, like a stiff phallus. Blaugast removed the dirt with the wooden face of his brush. He was still hot from the effort of rubbing and polishing to create the right shimmer when a breath panted close by. Filthy humor and giggling greeted him as a naked, hairy arm reached out of a shirt to touch his shoulder.

"Bravo, Ignoramus! — Do you see, that's more familiar to you than your *Cosinus Alpha* of blessed memory. Those are the calculations, you understand. You should stick with them."

Blaugast paused. The room, the furniture inside, began to tremble in a whirl. A rat's tooth, voracious, bespattered with carrion, gnawed at his intestines. He wiped the sweat from his temples, and, with his hand still holding the brush, soothingly stroked his eyes. Like a close-up in a movie, dissolved by memories, Schobotzki's grimace fell apart and distorted.

"It's you? — You?"

"Certainly. Does that surprise you? It's an honor for

me to come calling for occasions of 'sexual intercourse.' That Wanda is a piece of work. You've scored a hit."

He examined the shoes that Blaugast had dropped approvingly in his paws.

"They're stunning, these two. The crowning achievement of a classical education."

And when the laugh he attempted wasn't echoed by Blaugast, he brusquely pulled a tattered bill from his pocket, spat heavily upon it and stuck the paper onto the forehead of the motionless man. Complacently, he marveled at it for a moment.

"Wonderfully accomplished! — Once the prima fiddle in a gypsy band in the Land of the Aristocrats. Don't you know that old Hungarian tradition, from those rousing 'paprika-operas'? A person should be generous. And the week begins marvelously. See you, old friend! — *Vivant sequentes.*"

With a snarl and crooked elbows, the spook disappeared from the room. Splashing and snorting, the vulgar refrain of a song that Wanda mischievously hummed, crowned the morning's washing.

Blaugast stood motionless. The banknote, its soiled edge unfurling defiantly down his gaunt nose, hung on him like a jester's mask, a Mark of Cain for his estate.

VIII

During the night, opening up vast and merciless before him, burying his sleep deeper, more torridly than usual, deluding him with dazzling lights over gorges filled with the howling of wolves, Blaugast had a dream. A field lay in a solemn expanse, the sky monstrous, a horizon engorged by the depths. In the far distance, smoldering with shadows and rumors, the primeval wood, the Ur-forest. Blaugast recognized it by the fear that stirred him whenever he came across the word in the books of his childhood: primeval. This jungle was evil and mysterious: anxiety bellowing long and loud, drawn out from the throats of scavengers in the dark, confused and abandoned he groped night-blind, in a circle, clawing his fingernails into broken bark. With uneasiness and dread, he heard its murmur mixed with a familiar panting. Lust-filled rage in a padded cell — isn't this the way sexual heat panted when it attacked its victim? Profoundly unleashed, discordant and in upheaval, he suddenly understood what it meant. The Ur-forest was on the march. Like a flood and its breakers, it emerged higher, bodies pushed themselves provocatively forward, faces painted in piercing luminosity faded away cowardly in the crush. Blaspheming and cursing, a dreamy golden twilight, it moved closer, the hour at the end of time when a nocturnal specter bursts open like a cadaver with tempestuous mockery, stench, and despair. The Forest of the Damned was on the way. Its march immense, welling up in malice from circular eternity. There went women whose sweat had washed their lips of makeup, men in creased dress shirts, smiles glued onto their servile masks. Obscenities and breathing seethed vulgarly, the retarded giggled miserably; sighs, undermined by the unspeakable, impeded the feet of the marchers. — — — In front of all the others ran a woman. Her dress, grimy and strange, slapped about like a flag on her scrawny body. Her brow was cloaked in strands of hair loosely curled, her lower jaw, slackened by her lack of teeth, shivered unceasingly. Behind her the Ur-forest mocked and hounded; hands thrust forward out of the tumult, grabbing at the fleeing woman. And a whisper, unclear at the beginning, followed hard on her heels, scraping ankles sore from worn-out shoes, splashing puddles onto the wriggling legs of whores. A scream rose up behind her, relentlessly stumbling over the field, not letting her go:

It's your turn! You have to confess! — — — Malicious joy, incited, trampled behind her, vaulted a millionfold by agitated whispering. The Ur-forest had opened up, the shamed creature broke from the fold, the clamoring souls tried to suck her into their realm. — — — You miserable cunt, skipping so nimbly over pools of dung, stay and show us your face! — — — Do you really think you can escape? — — — Hoho! — hee hee! — — — It's your turn — — — With a heave that made the overzealous sway, the swarm suddenly stopped and raised its eyes to its quarry. The woman in front of them had turned around. From somewhere in the gray clouds a cone of light emerged and shrouded her entirely in fire. She stood, her emaciated face hardened, and raised her voice:

Are all who lust for a confession assembled? Is the tribunal that considers it its mission to condemn me at hand? Oh, have no fear — the matter will be handled with all propriety! — — — I'm not like you, I'm not stingy with filth. Are you ready to taste it? I know you, henchmen of infamy, unworthy servants of preyed-upon lewdness. You've humiliated me, you've spat at me, you've dishonored me, you were fellow humans in a world that disowned me. That was a world worthy of *you*. Do you know what a life such as mine looks like? Gagged, ravished, always in the mud, in the gutter, in darkness? Oh, no. You don't. You sat in your offices, rubbed your bellies against impressive desks, your thoughts stewing in the thick juice of boredom. But my thoughts? — — — Always ready to spring, shaking the inconceivable that enslaved me. That's the world. To be shut out of everything that illuminates and glows, smells pleasant in balmy gardens, resonates in concerts. Always to stand aside when the chosen few celebrate festivals, beclouded in cleanliness, to scrounge in the repertoire of acquired theatrics. Do you really know what that is, a whore's alley? The evening's black, glazed with ulcers, the room cold with a lamp mired in soot. One creeps along the houses slowly, amid the snow skipping dully between defiant lanterns, rain falling in the muck, haze lurking, a storm erupting between one's legs. — — — But that's not it, neither the hunger, neither the nights spent in the frost under the docks: It was awful that I was up for sale, to miserable hypocrites in a shitpile of misfortune. I, who came out of the chasms. Not that sin horrified me. There were those with depraved blood, angry, conned by their boundless yearning. Being of the same stock, shaken by their burden, I attracted them. There was one who dragged me by the hair over the floorboards before he made love to me, one who smeared my face with filth, who found great pleasure in insulting me. There was the man who came to my room in the evening to kill. I saw his face, the wishful torment of the deed. Pity, irrational pain had me trembling. Don't do it! Don't do it! — — — You're my brother! — — — Don't you see? This was the way of the man I loved. He came out of the night, assailed by ghosts when alone. When he kissed me, death hovered nearby. He was a loner, one the world had disavowed. He belonged to us, to me, to the guild. And you? — — — In the meantime, you've chattered about duties, blabbered grammar-school vocabulary, occupied your women at charity events with questions of etiquette. Not one of them knew my daily bread: the torture of sex, the pulse of remorse, a humanity degraded from crawling on the floor, love that goes to the dogs, the odor of midnight, drunkenness fizzling out unconsciously in sleep. But every one of them gathered up their skirts when I passed by; noble-minded and liberal, they kept the distance that was my due. But their husbands who wandered into the alley, they lost the inbred, dignified seriousness of their class in our bed of sin. They paid rent and lunch. I was the woman of their desires. — — — Then came the day God had reserved for me to spit before his image. The ground did not open its maw; the thunder remained silent before the hour of destiny. It was the day I strangled my child. Yes, yes, there you have it. That happens in this world, that's what people do, mothers with their hands. A child, right, is peaceful and sweet, should represent emotion and salvation. It grows up, is brunette or blond, called Walter, Heinz, or Hannah. Birthdays come, the cake's decorated with candles, the doll carriage has curtains of blue batiste, the rocking horse creaks in the room. But what's a girl like me supposed to do with a child? Is it supposed to see what its mother is doing, day in, day out, and with men? Is it supposed to cruelly fall silent, with its precocious eyes, even as the whispers fly around the school desks? One has given birth alone, without help, like an animal in the night. There it lies, still bloody, thin and shriveled, so tiny, so pitiful. Where am I? — — — What's coming over me? — — — Away with it, away before the landlord finds out, only quickly, for God's sake. It felt no pain, I swear by my soul, it only gulped a bit as I squeezed its little neck. Then I stuck it in the sewer. It was over and done with. The last thing to be seen was its arm, a child's arm with a tightened fist. I would have preferred to name it Walter, it was a boy, you see, such a beautiful child. And in front of the school I would have waited for him with a sandwich and a rosy-cheeked apple. I killed him, it had to be that way, he wasn't angry with me, my Walter — — — But you see: since then everything around me has made sense. Every morning — bitter-tasting like poison, and pale — dawning after nights that howled murderer! murderer! murderer! behind me — they all reminded me of humanity, that it tolerates such a thing in its midst. Mankind doesn't tremble, doesn't sway, doesn't fall apart lamenting; it conducts its business affairs, brags in clubhouses, dismisses the shame of heinous moments with pious kitschy phrases. I've hit the rabble in the flank, with an art that lures disaster from its hiding places. Then, I lit flames, infected desires, eagerly engaged with scoundrels. Then, I ruined their blood with the scourge, loosened horror from its dragging chain. Haven't you noticed? — — — How depravity oozed out of my street, glowing, sludge-green, from my embrace? I was on the watch, night after night, in the outskirts, the bars, under the bridge. I've served you as long as there was still marrow in my bones. Glitter and the faces of whores aroused you. I wasn't lazy, I've done my job. Power was granted to me to besmirch God's name through my trade: light intoxication in the darkness, the sting of malice, the splendor of the beggar woman — everything was mine. There you have my life.

IX

A pause, an unyielding buzzing in the ears, the surging of
the forgotten, resounded for several minutes. Sounds from
the depths, teeming vermin, threatened sadness. And again,
as before, when startled confusion flew from its undergrowth, the Ur-forest began to move. Feet stomping, fingers
clenched by mercilessness, throats longing for collapse,
vomiting, cackling, scorn, and grimaces. An unrestrained
chorus, a heaving echo called for the Judge. Through his
closed eyelids, Blaugast saw the wide expanse raging with
restlessness. Like the tongues of flames, memory overtook
and frightened him. It was a long time ago, twenty years or
more. Between now and then lay defiance, a guilty conscience. Was it not defiance that coaxed retaliation out of
the depths of time, out of the distance? — — — Blaugast
remembered. There was an evening, mottled with mold,
when he made a trip to the brothels with friends. Clearly, all
too obviously, he saw the bar, the grimy floorboards, the

bottle of seltzer on the table. The linoleum yellowing in shreds, with crumbled cigarette ash and tears. The landlord rolled up his sleeves, the clock with the sprung dial cracked. There was a creature, fleshy and muscular, pushing toward him. She came from humiliation, awful and hunched, smelling powerfully of cheap soap. Her manner, slimy like a jellyfish, disgusted him. Woman, what business do I have with you? But she stubbornly stayed with him, wouldn't let herself be shunted aside, threatened him with kisses. He raised his hand, the approbation of girls spurred his pride, the eyes of the jellyfish twinkled in defiance. — You don't dare do it! — He did! The slap whacked triumphantly. Hate bellowed at him. Ragged nails clawed at his face. The water glass, aimed in anger, shattered into pieces against the filthy wall. But the landlord was already upon her, restraining the violent woman in his grip. Enraged and cursing, helplessness froze her face into a mask. I'll never forget that, never, curse you! Whenever Blaugast was beset with scenes of slovenly, wasted youth, he remembered this hour in the whorehouse with shame and sorrow. It crawled to him out of the canals of the past, an unhappy creature that made him shudder. What was it that so frightfully knocked behind the doors, shuffled in the corridors, rustled underground? — Was it God who was near, whose knuckles rapped on his soul, and so conquered it? A hundred times he had regretted slapping the face of that woman, that he had even dared to punish at all. His life, always teetering on the edge of chaos, was not the sort to be elevated above others. Since that time, in the dives of the city, among the bars on the riverbanks, he had searched in vain for the woman, tortured by his intent to humiliate himself. Half-asleep, hot with ardor, he sometimes saw her image. It was a night when life ripped at its fetters, hail whipped abandoned streets, girls in the black corners of doorways sighed under the lips of men. She was leaning against the last streetlamp, freezing in threadbare rags with scruffy hair, aged, madeup, her eyes burning from hunger. "I'm the one who hit you years ago — can you still recognize me?" She couldn't. Her gaze, beseeching and lifeless, limped over him, fixing itself helplessly on his tears. And the sweetness of his desire overpowered him. He bent his mouth to the hem of her sleeve. He had at last found her. Gratitude shook his body, throwing him to his knees. — Blaugast bored his inflamed eyes into the darkness, where an angry primeval wood roared. The feeling was in him again, and he clung to it, shaking — that all was only fantasy, that everything was spiteful and lemur-like, with pressure in the heart and suffocation of breath. He didn't understand this life that could open, as if a door without latches, onto an impassable path. He saw himself as a young man in the doctor's examination room. His expression was serious, the shoulders shrugged and begged for forgiveness. "What's it going to be, Doctor, tell me — is it bad?" — "In twenty, thirty years, nervous disorders can sometimes set in. But it doesn't have to be that way. It's like a train accident, it can happen to anyone, you understand? — Naturally, it's better when one chooses not to travel by train! —" That was cautious, considerate, as cunning as an oracle. But it left gaping holes where the brood of the night might nest. What had happened? — The locomotive that carried him, traveling with red lights into uncertainty — had it landed in the abyss? — Why did he suddenly hear the distress call of the world so terribly, why did the grief of humanity ring in his ears, sirens of the insane, mothers calling to their children, the damned genuflecting? — I will never, ever forget that, damn you! — Guilt, guilt, guilt was life, guilt that rose up, delirious, in convulsions, to break down, tortured. How was it that many people grew up in good homes, took their exams, entered into marriage, were comforted at gravesides when they cried? There were cities with bridges, houses with a hundred rooms. People lived next to one another separated by a wall as thin as paper. Passions crept mischievously through the cracks, into the air laden with haze, extinguishing chandeliers. Boys, wrestling with the seasons of the psyche, slept full of melancholy next to criminals, the masters next to the slaves. Noise rose senselessly out of shafts, went unheeded. Blaugast couldn't fathom it. He saw the child-murderess, hung as if crucified, arms spread out on a beam of darkness. And a wind that imperiously split the expanse also ripped a passage into the Ur-forest. In the tumult retreating in tides before him, a man in a flowing coat with the face of an actor approached the motionless woman. He bent his proud head and commanded her: Cry! — And when she remained silent, her mouth warped in contempt, with a foaming grimace, he touched her with his hands: You're supposed to cry, Sister, you're supposed to cry! — Something inexplicable took hold of her, pressing her forehead toward his feet. Groaning, supernatural peril tormented her body — a torrent crashing upon ruins, a stream taking her life, whisking it away into the Unknown. There swam the nights she feared, fainthearted anxiety, songs of whores and dances, anger gnashing with crumbling teeth, her own dreams, jailhouse bars, laughter, flat beer stagnating in glasses, the accordion singing, obscene groping, the kisses of drunks. And when she cried, when her tears came, forgotten for years, buried for years, when in a whimpering fever she vomited dust and profanity onto the floor, the voice of the Messenger sounded, a voice immensely peaceful, a voice immensely tender: "Let the others have the world, Sister! — God has prepared His Paradise only for people like you." — She raised her head, looked at his mouth, the bitterness she exuded turned sweet. And while he continued to speak, gently comforting, about the young son at home, little Walter, her child, waiting for his dear mother, while in her heart heaven rose grandly, irresistibly, while the field became transfigured, the Ur-forest sank, the sun beamed over the open fields, Blaugast awoke from his dream. From afar, as the ringing of morning's bells slowly faded, he still heard faint whispers of the words that the accused woman, muted and distraught by the miracle, had stammered with the heavy tongue of those who pray into folded hands: You are full of mercy. The Lord is with you. You are blessed among women.

X

Following the dramatic, grotesque act Schobotzki performed at the reunion with his old schoolmate, Blaugast left the house. Whatever remained of his self-respect, slowly being destroyed by tears unshed, tortured lust and a residue that burned within, led him to flee. The last vestiges of a semi-acquired morality no longer his, yet to which he remained loyal, rebelled within his body. He left the flat he shared with Wanda out of necessity, left the corner of the room she'd granted him, the criminal deception of a crippled domesticity, to live among the homeless and tramps. With only a bundle of his possessions, he rented a bed in a basement belonging to a gang of criminals. The habits of his previous existence became irrelevant; all the compromises he'd made had produced the present caricature of a once eminent position, whose meaning had been lost through the process of his debasement. His tattered jacket was stained with scraps of food. He no longer shaved; his upper lip was covered in stubble as clear as ice.

Hat in hand, with the embarrassed pathos of the destitute, like an animal frozen on its way to the slaughter, he slowed the pace of traffic that crisscrossed the neighborhoods of pleasure and bourgeois prosperity. He was standing next to the movie house, where, after the showings had ended, dawdled a public satiated with senitmentality, and so rendered sympathetic to all forms of embittered beseeching. Blaugast begged. He did it reluctantly, with the pedantry of a civil servant assigned a new duty by his superior. The gloves he wore, the well-worn spats he still buttoned over his ankles as the unavoidable symbol of a haunting decline — all gave him the appearance of an actor following a director's cues. These people who'd groped their way up from the underworld of commonly coined emotions into the realm of homespun wisdom, the shop and servant girls who spent their off-hours illuminated in the glow of the screen, hesitated at the lure of his disguise. Still imbued with the cloying sweetness of the scenes that had just faded, pity suddenly revealed the gimmick to them, corrupting Providence, buying off vague assurances with payments deferred. The alms that Blaugast picked up in the gutter outside of those tender talkies were the most effective catchphrases known to the trade.

Afternoons and evenings he assuaged his hunger among the drafty feeding stalls where morose invalids slurped a quick meal at the repulsive tables of poverty. Sometimes in a soup kitchen, or else at a butcher's shop, he would get a tepid boiled sausage and then consume it in the twilight of a hidden passageway — a welcome addition to the bread crusts in his coat pocket; or else he waited with a mob on the steps of the Emmaus Monastery, impatient for the convent's soup. Here in the bare high-walled courtyards in front of the St. Wenceslas Chapel he had squandered his breaks as a Gymnasium student before the beginning of Sunday Mass, enjoying a favorite pastime of his classmates: sharing gossip and stories about the private lives of their pretentious professors. The roaring of the organ, the broken voices of the graduates that jeopardized the emphatic high notes of the hymns, came from afar, flooding irretrievably into his ears.

Within this examination of his conscience, a devout sensuality broke out of his past like a lost wave. As a boy, he sat at home with the well-thumbed breviary while the spiritual exercises of the days of Easter raised the monstrances, while sinful whispers swept among the stony grottos consecrated by remorse. Thou shalt not commit adultery. The threatening Law of the revered tablet arched above him, uncompromising, rotting and besmirching his ambition. No prayer of repentance had ever helped. Years of apprenticeship that had feverishly solicited his indulgence, years of travel amid the undergrowth of stunted seedlings — all rolled like a caterpillar, like the steel treads of a tank, over him and the meadow of his youth; the wildflowers and the fields of grass wilted in the tracks.

A fear of dangerous portents writ on the walls left its mark on the lethargy that had him in its grasp. There was the girl who once a week made the rounds of the offices and the conference rooms selling garishly yellow soap, toothbrushes, and fine-toothed combs. Though she was but a child twelve years of age, the neighborhood she grew up in had made her streetwise. The dented cardboard box from which she untied her penny articles, tubes and metal pots, was only an advertisement for the wares she really had on offer. The small room where the filing cabinet with the rotted lock stood impressively near the desk was typically overheated for winter, when this little girl slipped in and began to amicably chirp in praise of her wares. Her little dress was short, between the woolen stockings and her underpants her naked skin could be seen, burned by the wind.

"Aren't you cold?" he'd asked hesitantly, as the collar button violently, yet pleasingly, pressed against his throat. His pen impaled itself on the paper, strewing mystifying inkblots over the lines. His hand, suddenly failing him, sank limply downward, grabbing for the back of her knee.

"Not anymore, if you'd be so kind."

Her coquetry, meeting him so diffidently, made him bolder as she shamelessly unbuttoned her underclothes. For a short moment, flaming tongues of desire crept upward, nibbling brazenly at his jacket sleeve, leeching the sweat from his pores. Then it was over. What was it? What had he done? The glaring trap of the paragraph that protected minors — the statutory law — fell suddenly to the floor and loosened their embrace. He handed the brat a banknote without even first noting its denomination.

"Go!" he almost screamed.

She left. She disappeared in a flash, the glass door gloating as it rattled while she scrutinized her gain in the hall. But she returned. As soon as the following morning she was back at her station. Blaugast, neck pulsating, set the toil of daily work in motion. He was listless and sleepy, having had no breakfast. Rash haste, the encouragement of a secret wish, was generously paid for, had urged her daily into his presence. When he stomped up the stairs of the dark building, where the scorching foul breath of ratty furnaces fought in vain against the cold, where the clattering accounting ledgers and the dirty lavatories spoiled the day's work, her shadow darted around him, eagerly whispering the promise of gratification. He resisted, resentfully chasing the urchin back to the quarter to which she belonged. But the puppeteer behind the scenes was stronger than his resolve. Her withered face, smutty and impure, greedy to turn a quick profit, pursued him on the street. She ran after him, even when he would save himself with a quick jump onto a tram; she tracked down the flat he fled to, pushing craftily and with purpose through all sorts of barricades. Not until a weeklong stay in bed had made him invisible did this little interloper behind the wall give up her attempts to quarry him like a fox. His recovery was fortuitously accompanied by a blessing — he was rescued from evil.

For a long time, Blaugast was not able to recover from the shadowy fright of the girl's entrapment. This incident, trivial in reality, was reluctantly magnified in the glow of temptation, mutating into excess. He had been the wild game, the fleece hunted by the pack, and faith in the guaranty of his final escape tried his belief. Later, every now and again, behind buttresses, amid the throngs of pedestrians, he thought he recognized that pair of eyes lit with favor, demanding his consent, then blackmailing him for the requisite sum to keep quiet. The hypocrisy of his retreat lasted for seasons, and was not overruled by the resolve he was so anxious to maintain.

Once, when he had been a young trainee passing the gloomy, boring hours at work, a message had come for him that had similar effect. In the classifieds of the newspaper, he had come across an advertisement strewn with cryptic solicitations amid the numbers to contact, luring spies out of the market of love and into the niches of poste restante. Shadowy and abbreviated hints splayed themselves in an almost nauseous fashion between the lines. The result: an exchange of cravenly audacious acts, which under the guise of anonymity spared every restraint. The vagaries of the senses, muted by decree, the cannibalistic gluttony of unrestrained desires — all ventured into the Unknown only to return to him extinguished and abused. Until, with timid heart, he'd finally crumpled up the scrap that carried his name above the address, confirming the suspicion that would at times afflict him: that he'd followed a canary down into the mine, had become a disgusting connoisseur of alien secrets — by divulging the expected passwords in a hand disguised. Unverified had schemers picked up the scent. The skepticism of guarded suffering was no longer his own.

Costumed in the mask of a middle-class mentality, the threat that shamed him, that lay ready to pounce upon him in ambush, had not yet been made real. But the warning lingered, peering at him through door drafts, his companion for years to come. The regularity of bourgeois habit unwound into frays stranger than he had feared. And yet it was Woman, the disastrous weight of her seductive denominator, that had upset all his order, altered all calculations.

Blaugast gave this thought as he ladled soup in the forecourt of Emmaus Monastery among the poor, lazy, and sick. He counted the cobblestones that had scratched his shredded shoes as if they were the many tokens of a demystified world, the minutes, hours and days of a life transformed. Blaugast ate hastily, foam running over his beard and into the bowl, mixing itself with the food. In the gaps of loosely set stones, where the wind had worn away meager bits of earth, a dusty-green blade of grass sprouted. Like an unused manhole impregnated with inflammable gases, the abyss of memory yawned.

XI

The small suburban beer garden was full of young people, companions who had somehow come into conflict with bourgeois mores, and so who met together on occasion. Doctors who had just completed their final exams and were leaping into life with cynicism unspent, painters who had obtained their filthy humor partly from the pub, partly from art school, alongside writers and students. The sour wine they drank enthusiastically glowed in their veins and always led the conversations over obscure contemplations and then back into the harbor of a lewd anecdote. Every so often one of them tried to clear the way for a distinct point of view and to keep the discussion on track; but tradition was stronger and soon killed any such undertaking with a quip.

One evening in midsummer, the festivities lasted longer than usual. Midnight was already approaching when Blaugast parted from his comrades and set off for home through the pitch-dark Stromovka Park. These summer nights of twenty years ago were different than today's. War and atrocities had not yet filled all realms of the soul; one lived leisurely, lazed about, got drunk, and after sundown, when the bright stars made their appearance, a blissful sensuality was emitted from the earth's pores and weighed down the air with its haze. Blaugast carried his hat in his hand. A light wind brushed the hair at his temples, and the park smelled of distant pond water and damp bark. Behind him, from the houses he had come from, there echoed an occasional sound: a door slammed, someone whistled through his fingers, a dog barked. But the further he walked, the more the stillness enshrouded his soul in lethargy — it lined the way with mysteriously petrified trees, tamped down the low shrubbery into cowering clumps. Only the sand broke the silence, crunching loudly under his feet, his walking stick plodding forward with a muddled thud on the ground. These walks home were exactly what Blaugast needed in order to feel his life more deeply amid the monotony of the weeks. This silence after nights of drinking, lonely trips home as the carriages rattled through the reverberating streets, compensated him for the hours wasted in sleep during the day or else idled away at the billiards table.

Today he could not tap the feelings that he otherwise

managed so easily with the exhilaration of wine and laughter. Blaugast had drunk too much. He loved to manifest within himself that magnificent crossing between sobriety and intoxication, when the gravity of the flesh gives way to buoyancy. In the course of the conversations, filled with all sorts of jocular allusions to the unchaste, he'd recognized no limit. As a result, an annoying discomfort, with saliva bitter in his throat, now swelled up inside him; he fought against it in vain. He staggered, drove his walking stick down into the gravel, and squinted uneasily through his glasses. Off the path, where the darkness parted to an opening, he spotted something white. He headed for it, faltered against a wooden bench in the darkness, and there grabbed a girl who offered little resistance.

She was a young thing, not yet seventeen, and she peered blindly into the flame of the match with which he illuminated his discovery. Bit by bit, he brought out her confession. She was the daughter of a postman, employed as a day worker at a milliner's. She was promised to a young man her father disliked. This created all sorts of domestic scenes, accusations and beatings; her father's brutality was immediate, unrestrained. Recently, actually the day before yesterday, he had discovered her with her beau in the street and she dared not go home. Fearful of his anger, she had wandered about and then spent the night here on the bench in the bushes. She did not go back to the milliner's; instead, she stayed away the whole day and ventured out only once to the baker for rolls. No, she was not hungry at all, only tired, very tired — — —

Blaugast listened absently to her pathetic report. The wine and the conversation of the evening had agitated him. This stroke of luck came at just the right time, bringing him something he could play with. As well as he could see by the light of his match, the girl appeared to be cute and her teeth gleamed when speaking. He pressed her soft, round arm, carelessly groped her breast; it gave him pleasure.

"Come along!" he proposed. "I'll take you to a bed where you can sleep — ."

She was almost thankful. She breathed a sigh of relief and followed obediently, leaving behind her loneliness and fear of nightmares in the gloomy recess without so much as a backward glance. In front of them, at the end of the dark, tree-lined path, the street began, leading suddenly into brightness with its glowing lanterns. Blaugast stopped and scrutinized the little girl, who apprehensively hung onto him, and he lit a cigarette. She smiled weakly and shook her tangled curls as her narrow face sagged without emotion.

The hotel he brought her to was cramped and dirty. A dull, smoking lamp lighted the walls and the red nose of the chamber servant shoved itself intrusively into their pool of light. Blaugast sent him off with a tip and locked the door with the key. The drunkenness that had almost slipped away from him during the course of this adventure excited him once again, and evidenced itself in his thin, shaky voice. He pulled the girl, who, though intimidated, willingly obeyed him, onto the shabby divan and then slowly peeled her out of her clothes. She tolerated it without a thought; the more his lechery robbed of her, the more helpless she appeared to become, until she stood before him in the underwear of a very young girl. He lifted her up and carried her to bed. She slumped onto his shoulder and fell asleep, but he roused her, and she looked at him wide-eyed, kissed him mechanically, and hesitantly surrendered herself to his love. For a few minutes, her exhausted breathing became silent; then she pressed herself closer to the wall and fell into a deep sleep.

Blaugast looked at his slumbering prey with a little annoyance. He had expected the conclusion to be a bit more exciting and made a rough mental calculation of the gain and loss, weighing the pleasure against the costs. At least he had achieved his goal — the intoxication he'd been struggling with no longer oppressed him; only a light tremble ran through his nerves, and he blissfully gave into it. Carefully, in a surge of pity, he spread the covers over the girl. Her forehead, white and now shrouded, lay pitifully wedged between the pillows. His hand carefully stroked her head through the confusion of curls veiling her eyes. Then he blew out the lamp and with a sense of foreboding left the room.

• • •

The days Blaugast experienced were all the same, hollowed out by covetousness, overburdened by futility. Since that evening he had not once thought about the hat-maker, having put the encounter completely out of his mind. Every now and then, through a word or a movement, her gentle face would appear in his memory, but he brushed it aside. Only many years later did it return to take possession of him, this time never to leave. That was on one of the nights when his muscles were wracked with pain, when without hope for recovery he sought to comprehend the guilt for which he was atoning. Between the shadows flickering before him, the withered vanities, the cringing desires, the fields of stone that showed him how empty his life had become, the postman's runaway daughter suddenly stepped forward, leading him to ponder her in dismay as everything revealed itself to him. And while the sharp quill that tortured him lay waste to his flesh, while the night threaded itself out mercilessly between curses and prayers, never coming to an end, the forgotten face came out of the depths, alluring and sweet in stirring his conscience. In dark terror he understood the link between that encounter and his illness. Doors hideously bolted swung open, furtively waving themselves at him with suspicions and whisperings. The wanton desire that had ravaged his youth pressed hard against his bed, and the plundered sleep of the girl maliciously burned like tears in his eyes. Blaugast rose, spitting his disgust into his clenched fists until a nervous cough overwhelmed him, causing him to fall to the ground tortured, in utter despair.

XII

Blaugast walked along the benches of the park gardens and sold matches from an open box he had found in a dump behind the cemetery. The inventory of his merchandise, a half-dozen worn-out wooden boxes, did not decrease by this enterprise. The pensioners warming their gout-ridden joints in the sun, the destitute and the unemployed who squandered here their involuntary leave from work next to the mothers and the nannies — all left his meager collection untouched as if by silent agreement. Small change, which nevertheless accumulated at the bottom of his container, a profit seemingly mechanical without any obvious compensation to his customers in return, was payment made by unknown business partners and benevolent speculators. Because of his silence, Blaugast's outward appearance, which he now neglected unintentionally, took on its own peculiar character. More effective than any pleading, it invited charitable giving. The strange technique with which he stealthily moved his lips and averted his eyes, as the saliva-glazed corners of his mouth hardened to the words of his hushed appeal, was profitable for him, capital yielding interest and dividends. An ineradicable shimmer of elegance, a latent vanity, transformed him into a comical figure who mobilized the mockery of the street as if it had been provoked by the bizarre. The spastic goosestep of his uncontrollable legs, the result of the disease now consuming his spinal cord, his face, altered by the rigid dilation of his pupils, and the solemn rags he preferred as his wardrobe, earned him the moniker "Little Baron," which he would acknowledge with an awkward bow. The epithet was most commonly used by the children who ran behind him and by the habitués of the beer gardens and pubs, who welcomed the patient beggar with jeers and jokes. The deli owner and the merchants who stood respectfully behind their counters, their demeanors blunted by a lifelong servility to their customers, had their thirst for power and their suppressed despotic impulses unleashed by Blaugast's eagerness to comply with whatever conditions their generosity would impose.

"Little Baron!" some called gracefully whenever his stooped figure, humble and genteel, hesitated at the tables of the regulars. Now the moment had come to release the high voltage of all their horribly frustrated sadism to the harmlessness of an auxiliary lightning rod, to show off their superiority to the drunken women around them. One reached into his pocket and let the metal crowns sparkle in the light of the tablelamp for all to see. Orgasm, which suddenly and without resistance overtakes even the rich and powerful among us every time when the image of an inferior presents itself, electrified their humor.

"Little Baron, do the bird for us!" Then Blaugast would take hold of his nose with the fingers of his left hand, stick his right arm through the crook of his left elbow as if making a beak and hop on one leg and squawk. The sound he let out was suppressed, ridiculous, a gobbling whimper that added spice to the revelers' evening drinks, a cry that crushed itself in flight against the trelliswork, hoarsely cooing a final sigh before being stomped underfoot by the roaring of the spectators. This was the Little Baron's specialty. A bird imitator tolerated by lenient barkeeps and treasured by the jokesters, he had become a peddler of his own corruption. He now floundered through regions where the boredom he seemed as if called to dispel lay in wait.

In the nightclubs and in the back rooms of winebars and bordellos the situation was only worse. Here they'd discovered the tragic bond that tied the failed, miserable man to his depraved lusts, his untamed sexuality. While the champagne corks popped and shame stood outside the gates of the prison of drunkenness, the waiter, always keen to offer a special service, captured the wandering beggar at the door and brought him inside to display to the clientele. The half-naked women in the arms of their gentlemen had their fun with the bewildered Little Baron. Then, it happened. After downing a few glasses of schnapps generously given him, he was ordered to masturbate onto a plate in the presence of all for the succor of a meager fee. His groaning, and then his ejaculation — both served to guarantee a precious good time. That was the second specialty that brought Blaugast his honors, barricading, upon awakening the next morning, even the most impoverished of paradises with fences of barbed wire, generating sorrow in him and inescapable torture.

One evening, where the sooty acacia trees of a sandy courtyard feigned an oasis far away from the city, he met with Wanda and her bourgeois crowd under the veranda awning of a favorite brewery. They were all established, upstanding married men, clothing merchants from the shops of the Old Town, who squandered in her company the last vestiges of a decency that kept them from bankruptcy. One of them, for whom the hoppy stout had kindled a spark of self-consciousness, held the fleeing man tightly by the coattails.

"Call me a pig, Little Baron!"

Blaugast staggered. His lame legs cumbersomely shuffled to maintain equilibrium, but as his balance could not be kept in the grip of the drunk, he stumbled against the edge of the table. With spitefully knotted eyebrows, he squinted at his attacker's fat mouth.

"Don't be a coward, Little Baron, and just admit it! It's true, isn't it? — I'm a real pig."

Blaugast bit down on his tongue. In full view of Wanda, who eyed him vengefully, his throat constricted in seething anger against his tormenter. The man was sprawled out in his chair, his vest unbuttoned, baring his crooked fangs, stinking of sour fish and radish. His disdain for the chastisement, boastfully voiced, gave him a feeling of invincibility.

"Leave this one alone," Wanda scolded spitefully, snuffing out her cigarette in the pool of her saucer.

"He's spurting out what little brain he has left for cash. He's a dirty rat, and he's making me sick."

The reference to the disgrace that had dragged Blaugast into the depths came like the lash of a whip, sharply, with violence. A curtain ripped, bursts of light flashed, and Blaugast stared into the brightness.

"Of course you're a pig," he said to the drunk in an agitated tone.

"You're all a bunch of pigs, dogs, and bitches."

Applause accompanied the answer. Laughter panted out of their swollen bellies, vomit spewed forth, scalding hot and thick. Only Wanda, outraged, infuriated, remained belligerent.

"Who do you think you are? A prince of the sewers here on a business trip — — a shoeshiner for whores —"

Blaugast turned to leave. The rebellion against the treacherous urges enslaving him, polluting his life, was cut short. The gaping fire that had opened up before him, the grimace of his existence reflecting in the licking of the flames, narrowed again to disappear completely. His back hurt, and the darkness was breathing audibly. A couple of tables further on sat a group of Czech students who now greeted him jubilantly and wanted to see the bird. Unnerved, like a shipwrecked soul clutching onto a mast, exhausted by deprivation and terrified by the powers of hopelessness, he obeyed them and performed. The man to whom Wanda had spoken followed him, coming toward him with his ears abuzz.

"Sewer Prince!" he slurred decrepitly with his swollen mouth. The address came to him as if the last scrap of a disgusting caress, stomped upon by careless feet, dragged through puddles savagely and mindlessly, clinging to him as a permanent designation.

Thus rolled his wheelbarrow, devoid of brakes in gutters

dry of rain, down steep mountain passes. When by chance he loosened his gaze from the pavement, he peered into the display windows at the posters of cruise lines that traveled with their smoky trails and music bands to exotic destinations. He longed for the mountains and the blue of the Adriatic, a fossilized memory of a will he had once possessed. Some song plucked upon a mandolin while being warbled in a seductive if indiscernible Latinate tongue plunged the dull renunciation of his decline into turmoil. Or else he was suddenly confronted in the cool shadows of the archways by photographs that advertised dance cafés and a ladies' club with a jazz band, depicting alluring women in all types of poses. His jaw dropped and his mouth gaped. The breadbasket from which he had earlier picked crumbs, conforming to his transformation, was mildewing atop a pile of garbage.

After such days he would visit the gardens on the other side of the Moldau where the secluded stillness of the park paths guaranteed solitude to the hours of morning. Every so often the step of a lost walker crunched over the gravel. Schoolgirls rushed by with their red cheeks and the black and white uniforms of their anemic governesses glimmered through the foliage of the trees. Blaugast stood in the shadow of a bend overgrown with thick bushes. Like an animal become feral by an instinct deranged, he lay in wait for his prey. As soon as the bright red of a parasol, a fluttering skirt, or a checked scarf announced the approach of a female, he stepped out of his hiding place and exposed himself. With outstretched arms, sallow and defective, he blocked the path. The flight of the terrified women, their hysterical fear and repulsion at his image, brought him relief.

A game out of the netherworld that possessed him, this was the last pleasure enjoyed by the mentally disturbed wretch. The thorny part of his fate, the fruit of his passion, was obligingly opened, ripe for the end.

XIII

For a long time, Johanna hadn't been able to recover from the conversation that connected her to Blaugast. Something medicinal had surfaced, elements hidden from daylight had been recognized, understood, blocking passage between the twisted lies. She was no neophyte, no stranger in a world that gave her any right to asylum. As the daughter of a waitress whose first outings had been undertaken in the care of her working-class aunts, the term "parents" seemed overinflated to her from the very outset. The meaning of "father," especially, was divisible by the denominator of alimonies sullenly paid that left no remainders. The envy at possessions desired but unattained, as encouraged by lessons that caught her eye without fail in the abbreviated readings of school primers, soon gave way to the knowingness of an innate illumination: the abundant wastefulness of nature, which fritters away the fragrant pollen and flying seeds amid the air of the mountain desert — gifts at hand, for which the recipient finds little use, had nevertheless armed her with love.

As a schoolgirl, she had found her way back to her mother, sharing with her the attic decorated in such bad taste that it characterized an entire entrenched way of life: misery. There were curling tongs and makeup, silk scarves and worn stockings that peeked through the gaps of over-stuffed suitcases, along with postcards and hairbrushes. The lax atmosphere of an irregular daily schedule, which revealed no consistent system of afternoon naps and long evening walks, lulled her into a sense of security, though her vigilance remained intact.

Johanna very much admired the beautiful lady she called "Maminka" in the caressingly familiar Slavic term of endearment. When the now flaccid smoothness of her faded face had been brilliantly revived with makeup and her dull hair regained its golden cascading splendor, a wealth of curls flowing all over her forehead and temples, her daughter became enraptured by her charm.

"Take me with you!" she would timidly beg, intimidated by the rustling grandeur of gaudy evening coats, the polish of high-heeled shoes, and the silvery fish scales of her mother's little purse. "Go to bed, you runt! Maminka has to work for her money."

It had to have been a fine and elegant job one went to

so festively dressed, as if going to a wedding held in a fairy tale. Johanna lay in bed with her hands folded, gazing up at the winged cherubs sitting upon the feathery cloudbanks, and tried to pray. High up, in the seventh heaven, the Heavenly Father resided. Milk-white carrier pigeons rose out of the vision that oppressed her, carrying with them all human foolishness straight through the ether. Her childish message also went with them. Near the throne stood the catechist from school wearing a greasy tunic buttoned up with half-moons; he was snatching the whirling petitions with a butterfly net. When the Heavenly Father received Johanna's scribbled message into His hands, His whole face beamed as He broke into laughter.

"When I grow up, I want to be like Maminka. I want to go out into the street with colorful clothes and earn money. I want to wash my hair until it glows, and to paint my mouth with fragrant lipstick. Everyone ought to love me then. — Everyone."

God's voice resounded throughout the heavenly halls.

"Granted!" He commanded, and smiled benignly.

Unending cheer echoed immediately throughout the hall, shattered by the marble panels and the mosaics encrusted with diamond. The catechist with the butterfly net giggled respectfully, and the trumpeting angels in the corners rolled around with laughter, patting their chubby pink bellies.

Such was the slumber of little Johanna as her mother drank in nightclubs and stuck her earnings into her garter. Only later did she begin to understand. She already knew as a fourteen-year-old that depraved wishes were always the ones most quickly indulged. When Maminka came back from the hospital, ailing and shriveled, a painfully disheartened, tiny woman, the roles were reversed. She straightened the bed for the doomed and weakened woman, dropped the medicine like a professional into a glass of water, then lit the evening lamp. Johanna stood in front of the vanity mirror that for years had reflected the hairstylings and the gleaming cheeks of her mother when she prepared herself for going out. She was fastidious in paying heed to the laws of fashion. She plucked her eyebrows and suggestively teased a straw-yellow strand of hair under her hat. The lessons that had been illustrated to her in childhood had born their fruit.

"Good Maminka!" she consoled.

"Go to bed, don't worry. I'll get the money for rent."

It would have been a gesture of impiety to rebel against such a fate. Johanna, who had taken on the burden of her ill breadwinner, fulfilled her duty now with circumspection. The lottery ticket she had drawn, which Providence had saved for her, weighed as light as a feather before her desire for purity. Heartbreak gripped her once more, billowing like blood-colored smoke before her eyes, wiping the mascara from her eyelashes and inflamed eyelids. When her mother was driven away in the cab to be buried outside the city limits, a shamefully desiccated corpse, Johanna dug her fingernails into her fist, at odds with herself and Creation. But her sisterly kinship with the world, the wretchedly tattered realm of her mother, outlasted any inglorious death and survived even as she stood before the mound of the grave. The orphaned girl found her strength. Something unspeakable, a painful web of thoughts, an unsatisfied belief, demanded of her the mantle she faithfully took on.

Her intimate conversation with Blaugast had more than shaken her. The confusion of this gentleman who was wrestling with his demons required her care. She knew the wilderness that surrounded him, and it obeyed her. When his call for help came from the distance, seemingly smothered by the barking and ranting of devils, squandered life piled high as a mountain lay between them. Because Wanda had turned all away, Johanna would remain as his caretaker; the ragged, apathetic man would not leave her sight. Thus it came as no surprise that she reunited with his dehumanized being in the haze of a smoky coffeehouse. The staging of his scandalous deeds that whiled away the night hours for an audience of drunken pickpockets and homosexual hairdressers was the visible admission of those confessions for which Wanda and her whorish friends had obscenely hoped.

"Blaugast, what are you doing?"

Ghostly, like the tail of a comet, her address strafed and emasculated him. His sweaty shirt was torn at the neck, revealing the leaden filth of his chest. He raised his restless, wandering eyes.

"Don't you want to speak to me again about human dignity?"

He showed his blackened teeth, malevolently, like a caged ape tormented by spectators having their fun. The saliva staining his tongue and watering his darkened gums escaped from his mouth in a spray, coating her dress with its slime. Wild and ruthless, he spat at her, and the question he asked was tortured by revulsion: "What do you want from me? — What am I to you?"

The reproachful paleness of her face disgusted him. He quickly raised himself up, bored his fists into his eyes, cried out, fought against vomiting. His back, hanging like bent ballast under his tattered jacket, pulled him sideways. A coatrack came crashing down. His shins, smeared with blood, burned like fire. Blaugast fled. A spectacle of his own disgrace, he flailed along the walls, reaching the door. The fear of coming to his senses quickened his retreat. He abandoned the reward for his defeat, the lusts of absurd voyeurs, the applause of swindlers duped out of their filth, and escaped into the alley.

The encounter left them both filled with loathing. She came home silent, worn out by grief, limbs heavy. Her unappealing room, littered with Maminka's junk and her bed, standing at the ready, offered paltry greeting. The morose light of the goose-necked lamp at the window slid weakly over the wall to which she had turned. Something gilded, precious caravan goods covered in the dust of a sand-storm, nevertheless lay under the pillowy dunes like a secret hoard. The hero whom she had once created in good faith in her mind, the courtier and the hermit of her dreams, had fallen in among thieves. Naked and gagged, he had sat down among the stinging nettles, caterpillars and earwigs crawl-ing over his eyes, and stray dogs came to lick the pus from his wounds. Years ago, she had once possessed a book she would secretly read at bedtime. It was a novel from the world of the Turks, in which Templars read out the verdict of the Holy Tribunal; it teemed with rosary banners and Crusaders. The one with the silver star on his armor, who had been torn to pieces at the flank by hate and contempt — had he not been Blaugast? His name appeared to her writ in pearls upon bloody velvet whenever she had tried to resist its sound in Wanda's disgraced room.

Johanna fell asleep. The little sprout of self-imposed duty blown into her lonely sphere by a blissful gust of wind greedily drank up whatever tears she might have cried.

XIV

Schobotzki had rented a small secondhand shop near the Týn Church, wedged between the poorly-lit walls of the city quarters that until now had been overlooked by the corrupt egalitarianism of urban development. Here in the shadows of the medieval cornices, he ran a costume rental store, recognizable from the outside through the glazed eye of a miserable display window in which stiff wigs, mustaches under crepe-paper noses, and metal plates of rusted armor indicated to customers the type of wares available. Inside, the selection was not much better. There were uniform tunics with tarnished clasps, dented military helmets, horse tails the tooth of time had picked to pieces without any regard, ruffled collars, and Spanish overcoats.

During carnival, the ballrooms on Slavic Island saw a burst of activity. The Glove Makers' Ball and the coffee klatsches provided abundant conversational material for the domestics of the neighboring Neugasse as they fetched their beer, filling them all with great expectation and stirring them to intense bustle. Maidservants and housekeepers tried on farmers' costumes and suggestive disguises, and the mangy mirror opposite the shop's entrance twinkled in the dusky light for a few weeks with the profiles of tanned Gypsies and sharp-tongued rococo ladies. Chauffeurs and footmen who stopped off here on the holiday exited over the worn threshold disguised as bandits. Shepherds who had acquired their riding talents in the hippodrome scurried through the alley wearing holsters with pistols that no longer fired, inflating their masculinity and fueling their lust for freedom and adventure.

Spring and summer were dead seasons. Then, no one cared for the treasures that piled up here arbitrarily; only the street children who carried out their neighborhood mischief ogled with curiosity through the raindrop-stained panes. Schobotzki stoically noticed the slackening course of trade, the ridiculously narrowing profit margin of his ailing business. The glamor of these moth-beguiling costumes, faded knickknacks from his grandfather's day, the Biedermeier getups and the cardboard specters his rattrap housed — all masqueraded as a prospering concern. Papers rustled in the drawers of the desk positioned against the wall near the iron oven. Carefully arranged bank receipts, among them whimsical notes of debt prepared with date and signature, patiently awaited the inventory that, according to contract, and like clockwork, would unfailingly arrive. Empty promises, negotiated and agreed upon in corners, a labyrinthine playground for the vermin and mice, revealed the deals made under gas lamp as nothing more than a façade. Schobotzki, who captured the skittish spring tide of life for his private purposes in the oppressive atmosphere of the shop, had arranged confidential visiting hours for various initiates and aficionados. Wearing the expression of a benefactor who, as if through the eye of a worm, charitably judges the misfortunes of his clientele, he verified assets and extended credit to those deemed worthy. These numerous business transactions yielded high rates of interest, fleecing actors and dishonest civil servants, the common practice with which a fraud like himself fished for riches. To stand godfather to the pleasure that a bankrupted mind seizes on before the fall, to prepare its path, appeared to be his compulsion, a gift he much desired. Schobotzki was blind to any stones that didn't trip him up, to any nails that didn't pierce his skin. A connoisseur of his profession, he was a master of shrewd habits, a sexual predator gone wild in the bloody haze of the scent, finding pleasure in the perishing of his prey.

From time to time, a rumor of fraudulent accounting circulated among the public, which had been alarmed by the ruin of a merchant, the bankruptcy of a speculator, and the inability to find any causes for the various financial crises that now occurred in the neighborhood in rapid succession. A newspaper article reported the suicide of a bank employee who had been the very model of integrity. An industrial magnate poisoned himself, overdosing on Veronal. What precipitated these events was silenced by someone in the know and scattered far away from the secret chambers of Schobotzki's shop. The loopholes of haphazard laws were compliant enough that they could be cautiously widened, discreetly cloaked. The profit he gained from such knowledge proved itself agreeable, and very lucrative. It allowed him to support his extravagant nights, and it fed his competitive nature. He sustained the followers of his excesses with slices of sausage and goulash, and paid for the champagne ordered to satiate the goblins of his senile depravity.

In God's menagerie, the boozy costume lender was an exquisitely rare specimen, anointed in hell. In partnership with the restaurant waiters and the black marketeers of the erotic, he invested the extorted money in a strongbox of his own fancy, and made great use of the puzzling excesses of the psyche and its fatalistic combination of lies. Feeding on misfortune, he knew with the certainty of a sleepwalker how to track down his creatures — how to sow naïve fields of pleasure with afflictions, to pepper any venison that would please his palate. The suicide of workers fleeing impoverishment, the ruining of degenerates — these were the dessert fruits that he found the most appealing. Shaded by the wings of ravens, cowardly thoughts streaked his brow in wide furrows of accumulated malice.

In the nests of the nocturnal birds, where a lavishly dressed brood of owls and the daughters of bats and other flighty females parasitically lived off one another, he had become shrouded in an aura, transforming submissive superstition into a cult following.

Schobotzki knew from its heyday that generation of pleasuring amazons who, having long ago exited the scene, now served as charwomen of vomit-filled toilets, experiencing the ecstasy of the present only through its excreta. The memory this generation preserved was surreptitiously weeded and reseeded with vignettes of abhorrence. As closing time drew near, he humiliated many among them, exploiting their fear of being usurped. Even now, when he encountered a hunched figure working with a washpail on a neighboring floor of these shacks secretly protected from the vice laws and the closing-hour regulations, his jovial voice swelled with the arrogance of a victor; magnanimity was not the sort of item he ever had in stock. The joke he made of the ugly woman sounded to the ear like an incantation from a Faustian puppet tragedy.

Whenever Schobotzki's bony head and bent shoulders appeared in the doorway, the mood and manner of the troops he commanded, who defended the banners of his pleasures as if they were mercenaries, were conscientiously reported. The professional managers and merchants, dirty napkins clamped under their arms, the front of their frocks festooned with coffee stains resembling decorations worn by Bearers of the Order, bowed their bald skulls before him.

"A new arrival. Vivacious and extremely striking. Fair and innocent, too —"

Stooping in a manner both patronizing and brash, the guest of honor made note of the victim's description.

"Where is the young thing? What can she do? Does she have any talents?"

"The brunette over there. Barely a month over fifteen."

"I can imagine it. A child with curly hairs between her legs."

Then, flaring up, lecherously:

"Is she already infected?"

"Guaranteed infected!" the bald man bowed, sweating.

Like a connoisseur, Schobotzki knew how to identify the sexually transmitted diseases of the bit actresses in his little play, and he directed them all diabolically. The teenagers who fell into his trap, to whom he was good-natured and lively as he entertained them with brandy, were objects of his merest whim; their misfortune he skillfully exploited to the fullest extent. The illustrious hour comes with the morning chill — in this circle of duped Gymnasium students who had skipped their weekly dance lessons of respectability to study instead the true playboy style in the bar, here in his company.

"One more round for the road," he ordered from the waiter, and boastfully, even avuncularly, hissed through his teeth:

"And a lady with syphilis!"

A strange hero of delicate opportunity, a demigod of curiosity, an assistant to putrefaction, Schobotzki embossed his stamp on the nocturnal image of the city. Wherever distaste was reaped, scabby wounds broke open anew; wherever hysterical women became excited over rotting afflictions, he was available for their comfort. The confession of swindlers, who called on the police after their last drink to admit their guilt, the sighs of liars who talked themseves to desperation in front of drunken pranksters — all were a balm for him. He knew the paths taken by paroxysm, upon which a word or a shout could cause one's fall, and he trudged behind like a patient mule. Jealousy, strident confession, the stench of carrion — these satisfied his senses. Renegades of love, cocottes who bashfully transformed their pedestrian performance into astounding feats, the lost and the indolent — all lingered at his table. The heavy cross each had to bear was the gauge of his friendship and his respect.

Indeed, his calculations could never be off, even though the affection they craved was never his: he would grin slyly whenever his leather wallet displayed itself seductively in the depths of his coat's lining. Fear and greedy fawning licked at his heels. Defamation oozed out of the gaps, followed the wellsprings of his worth, surrounding the filth of his character with a poorly patched curse. No one would raise a finger against him or thwart his plans for the Patron of Bacillus. His money enchanted all propriety; soon, the starving and the infected would announce themselves to him as candidates for his services. Outrage whispered only underground, in the cancerous abscesses of remorse and nervous fatigue. It was an attack by a few of these clandestine deserters that would unexpectedly prick his aura — launching their camouflaged accusations against him, undermining the arrogance of his ascendancy with the pranks of wayward youth. The secret victims of persecution, tenacious adversaries, they announced their presence by night.

XV

It began with graffiti, garish and provoking, painted on the shutters the secondhand dealer closed at dusk. In the mornings, the brittle iron slats were smeared with haphazard writing, flaming red letters. Drawn from a conspirator's paint bucket, they denounced the demagogue within, gleaming critically in the early fog. "Schobotzki is an ass," the writing plainly stated, and the denizens of the alley took great pleasure in the inflammatory style of such defacement.

The owner, furious about the outcome of a session wasted at the card table, turned up around mid-morning with his key ring. Onlookers had already gathered in front of the store, as street urchins and women chattered about the grand implications of the advertisement.

Schobotzki hesitated upon encountering the spectators; he read the message and puffed through his nostrils. The shutters crashed as they snapped in their tracks, and the dawdling crowd dispersed. Shortly thereafter, a bottle of alcohol and a rag eliminated the irritant.

This occurrence itself would have been nothing extraordinary, simply an act of ingenuity and revenge from some snot-nosed apprentice who had crossed paths with Schobotzki and then made him the butt of a joke, stealing away silently after accomplishing the deed. But this act was only the prelude to a number of despicable scenes that seemed to be devised to degenerate methodically into a witch hunt, into a subtle and clever battle fought by invisible opponents. Irksome mischief and inventive mocking were soon busy outdoing each other. On the sign near the entrance an industrious knife had immortalized the insult "Dirty Pig," and so it had to be taken down. The postman brought Schobotzki anonymous postcards and letters smeared with slander and abuse. A package to be paid for upon delivery contained fingernail clippings and pubic hair deceptively wrapped in tissue paper. Or an ad in the daily newspaper revealed in emphatically spaced letters Schobotzki's address and the claim that he would buy damaged rubber hoses, wash basins, and enema bags at unbelievable prices. As a result of this maneuver, women eager to earn cash gathered in an excited mob. Responding to the glowing terms featured in the Sunday classifieds, they brought him shopping bags and suitcases filled with their attic junk. He was therefore compelled to take the trouble to reprimand the outraged throng, making it clear that even though these items had been advertised in print, it had all been a fraud. The commotion caused by the disappointed crowd in front of the shop reached such a crescendo the authorities were forced to intervene and disperse it with their nightsticks.

Yet the deceitful advertisement anonymously placed in the morning newspaper was not an isolated incident. Soon after, Schobotzki was looking to purchase cat hides, and then discarded dentures, or else he was advertising to pay for used trusses and unwanted girdles. The classifieds revealed his exact address to be the most convenient point of payment for all manner of unusable rubbish. Live dogs, regardless of size, breed, or temperament, were sought under his name. Free childcare services, the exchange of used phonograph records for new ones, and the recycling of old razor blades were all attributed to his interests. Idiocy, foolish squabbling, noise and gossip were suddenly robbing him of his peace.

The perpetrators' tactics would change whenever danger was imminent. A detective agency began snooping around for the cause of these disturbances. The cunning of covert operations gave way to violent street skirmish. The aggressors, who apparently knew the neighborhood well, launched their malicious attack by hurling cobblestones, broken glass, and other projectiles. Bars were installed on the windows at considerable expense though they were but cobweb ramparts against the assaults, which were undertaken with impunity as the vandals were protected by their cohorts in the alley. Cold contempt was Schobotzki's answer to this hostile tide rushing against him, damaging his property with makeshift slingshots. The false accusations he endured, the vast campaigns preceded by petty complaints — all failed to dent his obstinacy. So it was surprising when his stoic façade soon gave signs of finally being shattered by these nefarious tactics, which had been devised by the most vile intentions of his tormenters.

Whenever he returned from his nightly drinking binges, hungover, his tongue smothered in slime, he would pause in front of the shop door and each time found it smeared with feces. Cautious rogues, afraid of being discovered, clever spies and lookouts — all relieved themselves here. Whatever malevolent acts and harlequin pranks failed to achieve, the crude tricks of the misanthrope, who in taking the offensive now returned to tried-and-true methods, met with success. Schobotzki foamed. His annoyance, held at bay by a week-long effort in self-control, escaped him like steam, like a cannon shot into the air. The linden leaf that had felled the cuckolded Siegfried found a blind spot. The undercover actors in these war games encircled him, winning the first victory of their campaign.

The results demanded a repeat performance. The gang, seeking a way to undermine their victim's prudence, used their advantage unfairly, in a way contrary to bourgeois ethics. A pile of dung became standard fare on the sidewalk of the house that sheltered the hated shopkeeper. Schobotzki hired an obliging neighborhood cripple, employed by the community to shovel heavy snowfall or dog droppings. With shovel, broom, and sand the one-armed man gave it his best, but the persecutors' cleverness and tenacity always quickly trumped his efforts.

The police surveillance and the discreet skill of his hired detectives failed on this occasion, too; one group shrugged its shoulders, the other retreated, boastful and noncommittal. Schobotzki promptly renounced their employ in order to handle matters on his own. The shop, used until recently as a setting for his various wheelings and dealings and as an office, would now serve as his lodgings as well. He spent his nights on a mattress, still dressed, always ready to pounce, shaken out of his sleep by every noise that stirred outside. Steps, muffled voices, the murmuring of vague conversations — all tempted his vigilance. The walking stick of a drunk clanked over the cobbled street. He sprang up, threw off the woolen blanket, undid the deadbolt, and opened the door. The night air coolly entered his den, and the alley was desolate. Drizzle came down and wetted his disheveled hair. Cursing, he once again secured the bolt, climbed back into his foxhole and wrapped himself up in his bedding. Panting from the restlessness that impaired his breathing, he fell into a daze that lasted until daybreak. When he was awakened by a headache, frozen stiff, he was infuriated by the lost, irretrievably wasted opportunity, and by the stench of shit already creeping through the draft of the door.

It's hard to know with certainty whether it was just by coincidence that Schobotzki's rage was visited upon Blaugast's head, or whether it was by a mere error of judgment that the shopkeeper vented his wrath upon the weakness of a defenseless man. There are issues unfathomable to the observer: cesspools of destiny, hidden links of fate, the template of existence. Perhaps premonitions of dread had directed Blaugast's step, selecting him for ridicule from among the fallen. Perhaps he'd been purposefully deceived, polluted by the grief of being caught unawares in the alley where the befuddled man lay in wait, a lonely creature prepared to deliver his masterstroke.

Rusty metal sprang, clattering in the air. Schobotzki, malevolent and cursing, stood tall before the trembling man. Any unknown assailant, hastening away around the corner, and there shouting out a curse by way of a greeting, had no relevance to this fury, the full rage of Schobotzki's revenge. No mistake was allowed to spoil the pleasure to be had in a successful catch. Gaunt, tendons taut, his vulture arm reached for the terrified man.

"I finally caught you, you pig!"

The blows drummed down like hailstones, beating the tender flesh from Blaugast's bones and leaving him spotted with welts and bloody boils. He endured it all while still standing. As if the crucified Christ in the paintings of ecstatic Dutchmen, his crumpled body hung on the stake of the morning hours. His abused head dangled, weak and battered, until his chin rested limply on his chest. The gnashing teeth directed against him and Schobotzki's wolf-like gullet were the last things that frightened him, the last things he was aware of as he sank to the ground. Unconsciousness overcame him, releasing the urine from his brutalized body, dismembered by the verdict of guilt and its concomitant confessions. Was it a northern light that appeared, parading in the sky? — A meteor that had fizzled? — The face of God appearing behind a thorn bush? —

He was no longer aware of his almighty torturer's clutch at the nape of his neck, as his meek, desperate face was shoved into the shit, filling his nostrils and mouth, irredeemably swelling and decaying into ooze.

XVI

Life isn't all glitter, even for the fortunate. The earth on which we live, this home of audacious conceit, of games and sorrows, of fashionably blonde, mollycoddled dolls lying in their elegant carriages, of murderers and butterflies, autumnal roses and persistent hunger, has both its gates of Hell and realms of Heaven. There grows no hedgerow separating misery from eternal bliss. The lonely live among the blessed, all under one roof. There, at the gates to idyllic houses, burns the coal basin of Purgatory; the grape leaves fade upon the stone walls, the sighs of the perjured echo. But the pangs of love are indestructible, and are for everyone the same. In the ruined fields it sprouts as a stalk, full of yearning. It tearfully coos and flutters like a shamefully soiled brocade on the crest of those unaccustomed to hope.

When she chose her trade in the parlor above the well-trodden steps, Johanna had only a strip of clothing in her hands, God the Father's wretched coattails. She, too, had experienced what happens to women who offer up the adolescence of their bodies to the underworld of outlaws. Arrogant gossip, the stultification of those lacking in mercy, rubbed its muzzle against her. The ghetto to which she'd been banished seemed an undesirable home. Yet still she possessed an unspoiled nature, which she managed to hold and protect. The ingenious Eternal gilded her income and gave the metal crowns of her ecstasy a deified shimmer. Whenever the eyes of an imploring boy yielded to dreams of pleasure, masculine lips swelled and the creature in her embrace twitched, she was the mediatrix between him and chaos. The compulsion she lived on, groping its way up the stairwell, imperiously knocking on her chamber door, was an inescapable coercion. Johanna bore her burden with benevolence.

Innocent hands tugged at her dress. She slipped out of her frock, laid it shyly over the chair and let the shoulder straps of her blouse fall.

"Are you hungry for my breast? — Come, you dear man. — — Here I am."

And the blushing of a woman of easy virtue, which she had learned as a child in front of her mother's mirror, stood making peace over the moment, burying the shame of the sexes.

Revulsion and secret enmity lay like mildew on such relations, but in her world they were strangers, snuffed out by the excess she introduced into these relationships and by the revelation of an atonement abandoned. The stream of her compassion flowed warmly around perilous continents. Tattooed men and pirates sailed its waters, hoisted the flag and then capsized. Johanna's nature was most desirable; those enslaved, the outsiders and the irresolute, obediently circled her.

There was the silent one with the dark-rimmed eyes who smeared her crotch and her face with soot, lingered melancholically and left without a word of departure. The money he put on the dresser was justification for his deed, a silent explanation, compensation. There was the bearded one with the graying temples who brought a frog to her in a knotted handkerchief, which, while dressed only in shoes and stockings, she crushed with her heel. One fastened a silk scarf to her skin with golden needles. Then he ripped it away. The brightly colored blood flowed from her wounds like a little brook, refreshing his kisses. Johanna let it all happen. The plea voiced in childhood had been fulfilled: she'd become like Maminka. The wind in the street rumpled her colorful hat and her hair smelled of the essence of flowers. The responsibility rested upon her; the counsel of fate, absurdly and immodestly confusing her situation, was but a shadow she chased away. With omnipotent majesty, she remained uncompromising and noble whenever a peasant kneeled before her and found delight in her severity. Her maternal instincts yielded to insinuations suffocating in the searing air of overheated boiler rooms. Wide-eyed and detached, she greeted the man who came with a whip.

What the cultivated, cultured women, protected in their own respectable world, had ignored all their lives, what the righteous and the pragmatic never realized, despite their being skilled in all aspects of everyday life and preoccupied, too, with the maternal duty of upholding an untainted reputation within their sorrowful houses of cards — this came to Johanna as a gift accepted without hesitation. She looked over the shoulder of the Heavenly Father, Who castigated His Creation with scorpions. Pulses droned like the hammering of an anvil. The parched Earthly realm became a jagged expanse of volcanoes long-thought extinct. It was not easy for a woman who dared to explore uncharted territory with only a lantern to guide her way. Often the dark engulfed her, and she wept.

What had transpired between her and Blaugast was unspeakable, carried no name. She had deciphered the runic script of his anesthesia, wrapping herself like a woeful widow in the gauze of his confidence. Often it came to her like the melody sung by a child gazing at his kite flying high over harvested fields. Then she brushed the hair on her forehead into place, looked around her room — the song of praise fell silent. She took hardship, anxiety, and animosity upon her shoulders and would not allow herself to reflect upon it. In that book, illuminated by the lamp of her girlhood, there had been talk of the stars, heavenly bodies and moons that rotated around the mass of earthlings, forever surrounding them. Her lot, which was both command and gift, was to whisper paid lines, to pacify the lost, to receive the vilified into her bed. It never entered her mind to quit this path and to return home to clean the oil lantern for the benefit of those still unsullied.

This gift a fairy had left behind in the cradle, shamefully guarded like sparkling jewels, stood in opposition to the laws governing those of her ilk. It seemed to be a truth as paradoxical as it was absolute: Johanna the streetwalker understood loyalty to be the talisman of her existence. In aid of her femininity, amid the flightiness of those around her, she was the one stable core. She was the dot on the "i" in the structure of the alphabet, in the bill of sale for the illusions she offered. She was the very slogan to which she held fast, the tabernacle in the chapel and the beacon on the lighthouse. Blaugast was seduced by her loyalty; it worked invisibly in him even as its foundation crumbled, as he remained without shelter, the lowest among the living.

It was like a war. A regiment sets off to the front amid jubilation and handkerchief-waving at the train station. Horns blare, flowers flutter out of all the windows, the soldiers sing. A young, handsome officer rides ahead upon his decorated horse. His young wife, still sore from the kisses and caresses of their wedding night, is caught in the crowd of curious onlookers, mothers, and gossips. She can't reach the great man, no matter how far she stretches out her arms. Her tongue is paralyzed but her pride blazes fiercely, like fire releasing from its furnace. And even when they bring him back after months of promise, after years bogged down in the stink of latrines, crouched in a bunker, no matter what has happened, she cannot regard him as a frightened cripple, nor a formless piece of meat out of the slaughterhouse of disgrace. The hot flames that burned at departure return. The fear of harrowing events and artificial limbs divinely go up in smoke. The victor has returned, the archetype of yearning, the hero on horseback. This was what Johanna felt when thinking of Blaugast.

She had recognized him at once when he turned his face to her, surrounded by his nemesis who wore chain mail and the Order of the Golden Fleece. At once the dead had become the living. A gate opened and an assault of storms so pummeled her limbs she almost fell to her knees. So it had remained. Indeed, it was difficult for her to rescue him from the teeming misdeeds that had crushed him — visible in the fallow land, in the confounded fields of winter. The wheel ruts of his humiliation were embedded in weeds frozen under the sedge. The Indian-like cunning of his depravity rendered her help futile; it deceived her and led her astray.

There was no room for doubt, as much as her patience had failed her in childish protest. Blaugast had slipped from her grasp. He was on his guard against the divine, hanging on her burden of sins like a glittering bauble. By the grace of her presence, she endangered the void into which he had sunk. Under his shy eyelashes kindled the spark that inspired her awe, as long as he had remained strong. Now it was too late. The pervasive stench of his flatulence left him gasping for breath. The unspeakable had been committed against him at Schobotzki's doorstep; he was as an animal abused. Awake, his consciousness having returned to him in irregular waves, he was lying on his stomach in the dust of the street, a man mired in filth, spat upon and beaten, his life seemingly done for. Eyes bloodshot, body torn and violated, he came back home at morning light. The sun glimmered dreadfully. Its rays danced through the shattered windowpane in the corner above his pathetic cot.

"Beware of Philistines," rang the wake-up call he no longer heeded. As he began his daytime sleep, broken and debased, Johanna was suddenly afflicted by a despondency that unexpectedly overwhelmed her. She wiped her impious eyes with a handkerchief as emotion plucked her heart to pieces like the wind scattering the fluff of a dandelion.

XVII

Blaugast's illness broke out horribly in the days that followed. It not only violently transformed his physique, but, like unsightly cracks in a mirror, it deformed his reflective psyche as well. His accursed legs lost their footing, slithering uncontrollably and torpidly in all directions. His bloated body, hanging disfigured from the shoulder blades like a rumpled sack, groped and shuffled itself along the walls. Fitful pains wracked and warped the pit of his stomach, back, calf muscles and torso, as if they were in the grip of an invisible vise. The satanic, blatant distortion of the world was a nasty side effect. The unspeakable asserted itself in the spirals of degenerated nerve fibers, in the stimulation centers of his cerebrum. His morbidly confused mind and paranoid anxiety were shaken out of the lethargy induced by the alcohol, as by the morphine dispensed in the bathrooms of louche coffeehouses and the cocaine snorted from ragged paper bags.

At first the hounding of his persecutors rose up out of the buzzing that hovered over his bed. They were the bosom companions of disjointed ideas, of thoughts that had slipped away — the estates in which they frolicked he had long ago squandered as worthless. Skunks and warthogs sniffed the urine-soaked sheets, saturated by the bladder he could no longer control. Vermin swarmed over the garishly green-washed walls: beetles, disgusting woodlice and spiders, whose swollen bellies streaked watery tracks on the mottled plaster — — emissaries of an inflamed imagination that conjured up his boyhood. Or the *Seifentier*, that mythical werebear, pawing at the doormat that lay like a rumpled blood clot beyond the door draft — all remnants of a past that no longer spoke to him. His skull, covered with shaggy hair, cowered angularly amid feverish images from a time in which all manner of monsters, the mutilated and disgraceful goblins of night, would dwell in the fountain of his childhood. There was the wolf with the ghastly gullet, the pockmarked doctor and his aunt with the whooping cough. Pompuwa, the wooden Toy King in the brown cigar box, reigned again — despite having been decapitated by throne-hungry noblewomen. When the wick of the kerosene lamp flickered and smoked behind the bell shade, when his mother recited vespers from the well-thumbed breviary, the Negro came to visit. Blaugast relived it all.

Subject to the judgment of a miserable condition, it happened that he would recognize their faces in broad daylight. In the alternating currents of traffic, huddled together on the pedestrian islands of crosswalks, they all stood ready to grab him: the wolf, the wooden prince, and the werebear from the Steppes. Leading them all — Schobotzki. He was the most corrupt, the most evil. His long teeth smirked in every store window, appeared as a mask in the crush of electric trains, and rummaged in the solitude of the quiet streetlamps burning in the city's suburbs. He was the devil incarnate, and would stop at nothing — the nemesis, a man from the depths. He was preceded by a fear so harrowing it peeled the marrow from Blaugast's bones, that they cracked dissonantly, congealed like saliva in his mouth, and blew like a tempest over the back of his neck. "Schobotzki" the horns of buses blared. Loudspeakers hollowly trumpeted his name. The pealing of church bells and the whistle of factory sirens called out the syllables of the name he had so laboriously evaded, only to encounter it again and again.

"Beware of Philistines! — Attention! — Scho-botz-ki!" What he ignored in his apathy was no longer the order announcing an attack, or news from afar, but the fanfare and loud tumult in the near distance. He had to gather all his wits to make his escape.

The fragments of decay left over from the day's toil, the

sexual exhibitionism and the begging in the streets, all at once became trivial in light of the task that was suddenly confronting him. Blaugast had to save himself. The remnants of his trapped existence were threatened, the misery of a life stranded at stake. Out of subterranean crypts and bottomless passages came the enemy's call. They must never seize control of him, he must never completely fall into their clutches. He had to employ wiles against wiles, today here, tomorrow somewhere else, using his own designs to frustrate, patron of his own escape. What did it matter that hunger had him in its grip? The one whose very name he was loath to utter had availed himself of his slumber — the sleep of a vagabond — as a test of his devilry. At the moment Blaugast's vigilance waned, a voracious worm was introduced into his intestines to consume his juices and burrow against his stomach wall. Or was it a rat that had bored through his anus and into his bowels, a slimy rodent, or a weasel thirsting for blood? —

"Beware of Schobotzki! Save yourself, Blaugast!"

What happened now was unquestionably the worst, incomparable to what went before, unsurpassed thus far by nothing. There was no retreat to which possessions could be abandoned, where one threw his knapsack into the field and relinquished his only weapons. Fearful stumbling into shell craters, a panic-stricken alarm and absolute desperation.

Blaugast did not dare return to his flat. His miserable nest was known to the bloodhounds, and it would have been reckless to entrust his salvation to a mere rusty padlock. What would he do if one of Schobotzki's whims were to render him defenseless, if his claws grabbed hold to strangle him? Would it not be better to go into the maelstrom of the city, surrounded by the twinkling of lights, and there share in a more supreme power, Who would take even the most humble into His care?

Thus Blaugast, who had suffered the most evil at the hands of society — a society to which he had become a pariah — became cut off. The circuitous path, whose violent momentum had whisked him away, now brought him back again, to the beginning. As a vagabond, shrunken and weak, he slunk back in, insinuating himself again into the great hustle and bustle, where the monotone singsong of newspaper hawkers drowned out the warnings that nipped fast at his heels. Careless pedestrians walking in lockstep crashed into him. Those in a rush towed him along. His nostrils sucked in the aromas of the food vendors and provided him nourishment. His debilitation, tormenting at first, now comforted him like a blanket. But in the swell of the city, the degraded body that wished to escape its executioner became a porous grid whose contact cable had been severed. Typhoons raced out of storm-swept sectors, whirlwinds of confusion washed overboard the security of his delusions. Then he stopped at the edge of a block of tenements, where the bright lights of advertisements flashed like fire across the façades. Alone amid the turmoil, dehumanized, he was defeated. In the display window of a clothing outlet, the friendly waxen face of a mannequin selling a man's fur coat bore the grimace of the murderer, ghostly impure, familiar with original sin. The red and green painted disc of a yo-yo danced before his eyes. The movable wheel remained tethered to its track — such was its fate.

Blaugast turned around with his arms raised. The worm chewing at his navel extended its mouth and greedily bit at his heart. The road glistened monstrously and heaved like a narrow trench of death between the barking of machine guns. The gloved wave of a policeman, who guarded his Last Judgment like an angry foot soldier, was unable to stop him. The breath that scratched his throat hung sourly in his mouth and pumped his roaring lungs dry. His breathing came in mountainous waves, encircling him, finally bringing about his demise. His feet were leaden. The car whizzed around the corner; the driver's angry eyes flashed as large and as wide as saucers, and he pulled the hand brake a second too late. The driver cursed and scolded with malice as the blow threw Blaugast aside, sending him tumbling through endless caverns with a strange lightheartedness down to the last stop of his purgatory. And there was no one present who could tell him the truth: that the accident was Fate's secret decree, revealing itself as an epiphany, that the passenger in the car was actually Schobotzki, who, annoyed by having to stop at the scene, rolled down the window and gawked. Next to him on the upholstered seat leaned Wanda, looking indifferently as passersby gathered around the careless pedestrian. A policeman pulled out his ledger and wrote down the addresses of the witnesses. None of them knew who the unfortunate fellow was. Schobotzki and Wanda did not recognize him either amid the crush of the crowd.

One person came forward voluntarily, submitted her information, made her claim known. She unscrewed the glass stopper of a bottle she carried in her makeup bag and rubbed the forehead of the unconscious man with its contents while her hand supported his limp head. A premonition had brought her here — an imperceptible, instinctual quivering. When Blaugast raised his eyes, he sighed in astonished recognition. It was Johanna who bent over him.

"Are you injured?" asked the policeman. "Can you get up?"

He wanted to, but was unable, and so answered in the negative.

"Where does this person live?" inquired the man in uniform, turning himself harshly to the girl.

"Bring him to me. I will care for him. He's related to me."

And her face, scarred by the weariness of the world, brightened now like a window.

XVIII

Blaugast lay in the corner, in her dead mother's bed. He was here to stay. The accident in the street had left no visible marks; it had, however, injured his spinal cord and robbed him completely of the use of his legs, which even before had been practically immobile. Without protest, like a bale of hay mowed down by a scythe, he let himself be carried into the loft's closet that would remain his charitable home.

Johanna had the alcove housing the cripple boarded up by a carpenter. Visitors dropping by to atone for the fleeting pleasures of her willing embrace sometimes heard a muffled chatter, the babbling of a muddled dream from behind the wooden boards.

"Who's next door?" they would ask dryly, annoyed that someone was eavesdropping on their intimate, carefully guarded confessions.

"There's no one here to bother you," Johanna placated them. "He's a good man; there's no need to become distressed about it. It's only my ill brother."

In addition to her daily tasks, this elective service weighed heavily. She washed and cared for the cripple, bathing his cold, sweaty skin with vinegar. Whenever the weather would suddenly change, it caused him pain, making nighttime a hell. She sat next to him when, in his delirium, he cursed the crucifix hanging on the opposite wall; she sat next to him, laid her fingers on his temples, stroked his hair. From the Bible she read the story of Job, who squatted in the ashes, covered with scabs, and scraped his festering wounds with potsherds. She read how his friends observed him as they wept bitterly and rent their garments, how his laments cursed the day he was born, and how it was then announced at night: A baby boy has been conceived! Her voice stumbled at the message from the Psalms and at the wisdom of the preacher. An angel spread its wings, and Blaugast fell into a slumber.

Then, the beast was in his abdomen again, menacingly digging its claws into his bowels. Like a nurse, Johanna had to fetch the bedpan and prepare an enema, raise his hips from the cushion, turn and clean him. Such activity did not dampen the spirit of her appointed legacy. Without her noticing, the days slowly submerged into a realm far removed from the mundane — a realm she had hungered for her entire life.

The money rewarding her kisses lost its profaning

nature. She brought home calmative medicines, tablets in gold-colored cylinders protected from the odors of the room by cotton wadding; Blaugast obediently swallowed. She bought fine foods: sugarplums for his ravaged appetite, seasoned fish and exotic fruits whose aromas appealed to him. Red-sealed bottles from the Mělník vineyard emerged from the shopping bag the salesman had filled for her. The small, round-bodied bottles stood like friendly inkpots on the set table at which she fed him. Blaugast took a banana and peeled it. From under the thick, leather-like, spotted dress emerged the center, presenting itself as soft and as captivating as the body of a naked woman. He moved his tongue over the flesh and tasted it. Now he felt safe. What else could happen to him? And where was Schobotzki? His fear melted away, disintegrated like medicine on a spoon, comforting, assuring. Now he was safe. He took small sips of the fragrant red wine.

The grumbling in the street came up from below, like the ocean surf beating against a coral reef. It came from the distance, and here was finally shrugged off once and for all, now rendered powerless, harmless. An asthmatic motor clattered and coughed as evening made its rounds, polishing the slats of his strange cage with its reflections. Blaugast was alone much of the time. He lay on his back, his hands folded over his chest, waiting. Johanna had to capitalize and double her profit. In the soldier bars, in hostels of dubious repute, she flapped her skirts sensually. The income she made was enough for two.

Her worth was increased by the passion with which she offered herself. She pleasured men with deceit. Her heart went numbly and yet amiably upon a lonely path, but the fiery heat of her blood ran like an ecstatic wave over her body, which pleased her partners. She had to take what life dealt her: profane presence, boundless surrender, and the prison of dreams. Keeping watch at its stone gate was a wonder that never betrayed.

When she returned home, frozen by the wind, harried and exhausted, she smoothed her tobacco-stained dress over the clothes hanger. Blaugast was quiet, mostly. The time before daybreak was his most agreeable hour. Stewed in the exhaustion of his nightly drink, his breathing rattled stiffly. Johanna listened a bit, changed girlishly into her nightdress and scurried under the covers. On occasion, Blaugast heard the lamentation with which she extinguished her lamp. In his light sleep a shapeless whisper blew to him — the word with which she defended her charge.

"Johanna!" he called out in the dark.

"Say it again, Johanna! — I beg you, tell me. Am I your sick brother?"

Encarcerated within the brilliance of a star that had

never dared turn to love, the answer came resoundingly and
without fail:

"Yes, Klaudius Blaugast, you are."

Afterword

After attending a reading given by Paul Leppin in 1933 from his yet unpublished novel *Blaugast*, which was originally titled *Der Untergang* [The Decline], Max Brod had these words of praise: "[The novel] certainly belongs among the most unique, the most genuine and authentic that German literature has produced in recent years. Despite today's unfavorable circumstances, it will one day, sooner or later, fight for and win European recognition." Brod was not the only one who held Leppin in such high regard. At the time, most writers and artists in Prague — Germans, Czechs, and Jews — agreed with him. This admiration was perhaps best expressed by the brilliant Czech essayist and translator Pavel Eisner (who was the most influential in bridging the divide between the three cultures that made Prague such a unique city) in his essay "Prague as the Fate of a Poet" in *Prager Presse* (1930):

At the time of Czech Decadence, with which he had an affinity in his depiction of dark spiritual derangements, but from which his naturally unaffected disposition and passionate blood kept him apart, Paul Leppin, senses greedily receptive, absorbed all the poisons present in the atmosphere of Prague, all those specters avoiding the daylight, and captured them in his books with an ardent single-mindedness and intensity that only Gustav Meyrink was close to achieving. Leppin's prose presents in the purest form the traditional experiences of a German poet in this seemingly completely familiar but at the same time strangely unfathomable Slavic city, from whose feverish hallucinations he invokes his artificial paradises and infernal chasms.

Although referring to Leppin's earlier writing, Eisner's remarks succinctly capture the essence and importance of *Blaugast* as well. The novel, however, was doomed. As Brod had hinted, the political climate did not favor such a book and would prevent its publication. Nazi Germany would occupy Prague, and Leppin was not the only writer to see his work fall into oblivion. A last flicker of hope came in 1938 with the publication of *Prager Rhapsodie*, two small volumes of poetry and short prose, in which *Blaugast* (now subtitled "A Novel from Old Prague") was listed as forthcoming. When it finally did appear, in 1984, Leppin had been dead for nearly four decades.

*　*　*

After the Communists came to power in Czechoslovakia in 1948, Prague German literature was suppressed as decadent, bourgeois, and dangerous. A reevaluation of the past had to wait until the thaw of the early 1960s. It began through the efforts of Eduard Goldstücker. He initiated the first two literary conferences, held in the north Bohemian town of Liblice in 1963 and 1965, that led to Franz Kafka's rehabilitation as well as a new interest in and, as a consequence, research of Prague German literature in general. The seminal lectures and discussions of the second conference were collected in the volume *Weltfreunde* [Friends of the World],* which became the foundation for all future research and led to a number of theses and dissertations addressing this forgotten literary and cultural past. Leppin's rediscovery can be credited to Božena Koseková's 1966 master's thesis (written in Czech). It was the first extensive overview of Leppin's life and work and it formed the basis of her contribution to *Weltfreunde*, "Ein Rückblick auf Paul Leppin" [A Retrospective of Paul Leppin].

Around the same time, I and other young German literary scholars at the University of Basel in Switzerland first encountered Leppin through the study of Else

---

Weltfreunde. Konferenz über die Prager deutsche Literatur, ed. Eduard Goldstücker (Prague, 1967).

Lasker-Schüler's poetry, and we wondered who was this bard of Prague, so admired as a close friend by one of Germany's greatest poets, yet whose name we had never heard before.[*]

Extant references to Leppin's work were meager. Taking a research trip to Prague was the obvious solution. And luckily the "Prague Spring" had just set in. In January 1968, Alexander Dubček was appointed First Secretary of the Communist Party of Czechoslovakia and began a process of tentative democratization and liberalization known as "socialism with a human face." Young western scholars were welcomed in Prague, but the research conditions they found there were poor. The few copy machines that existed were usually broken, or invariably out of paper or ink. Many of the needed books were often not readily available anyway. They were stored in various locations (often in some castle) to which a library van was dispatched at infrequent intervals to fetch the desired material. Research, therefore, demanded patience. As possibilities for photocopying or making microfilms of archival material were limited, much of the research involved copying the various texts by hand. Many manuscripts, typescripts, letters, articles in newspapers as

[*]Lasker-Schüler called him "King of Bohemia," and in a short essay from 1908 in praise of his novel *Daniel Jesus* (1905) she begins with striking imagery: "Paul Leppin's *Daniel Jesus* ascends before me, a huge angular vampire wing with the eyes of an apostle."

well as anthologies, whole dramas and novels were left waiting. It was hard work; fingers cramped. In retrospect, sitting in front of a computer today and looking on the screen at manuscripts that have been digitized in high resolution, it is hard to believe that anyone would spend hours and hours copying archival material. Only my handwritten copies of the better part of Leppin's papers and a few photocopies of very poor quality, now stored in a row of file folders and ringed binders, bear witness to these times, proof that these recollections are not simply a bad dream.

But these memories are also filled with positive images. The personal support of fellow researchers in Prague was wonderful. They selflessly gave help whenever it was sought. They opened their private archives and libraries, and they made their own research — which was often still in progress — readily available. They were always willing to provide information and to aid in overcoming bureaucratic hurdles in the laborious process of uncovering biographical information hidden in the drawers of public offices and town archives. My Prague colleagues were teachers as well as friends, always forthcoming with tips on to what to do and what to avoid, where to go, where not to go. The contacts they provided included the names of Leppin's relatives and former friends living in Prague and Vienna. Especially important for the completion of a first sketch of Leppin's life were Marianne von Hoop, who played a crucial role in Leppin's last years, Leppin's favorite niece, Edith Fellner, neé Walter, and the family of Leppin's nephew, Zdeněk Leppin. They shared photos and letters, told stories of past times, and made me welcome. And these memories remain vivid to this day.

Leppin's literary remains, including *Blaugast*, had been saved by accident. Supposedly, the papers were found on the sidewalk in front of his home after the war, discarded as trash. Someone, whose identity is unknown, recovered and deposited them in the archives of the Museum of Czech Literature at Prague's Strahov Monastery. Unfortunately, no official record of this "donation" exists. A few additional manuscripts are now at the Deutsches Literaturarchiv in Marbach after having been donated by their former owner, Marianne von Hoop, to ensure that Leppin's work would not be lost and would perhaps one day be rediscovered.

The research conditions of those first months changed radically when a frosty winter followed the Prague Spring. In April 1969, Dubček was replaced as First Party Secretary and the Gustav Husák era began, what became known as "normalization." Suddenly, even public archives were closed or restricted. Documents were no longer available to researchers and special permits needed to be obtained from the Ministry of the Interior to access them. Colleagues and friends did not dare speak openly in their own apartments. One went on strolls through the alleys of Prague and sat on park benches to discuss ideas and exchange information. Rooms were generally assumed to be bugged, letters remained unanswered, colleagues lost their positions or were given early retirement, some went into exile. Further research seemed almost impossible, and interest in Prague German literature largely declined. In the West, publishers considered putting out editions of such work too financially risky.

There were plans to include *Blaugast* in an omnibus German edition of Leppin's major novels. After many years of negotiations, it was finally announced in 1982 under the title *Blaugast und andere Erzählungen* [Blaugast and Other Tales]. In addition to *Blaugast*, it was to include the short novels *Daniel Jesus* (1905) and *Severins Gang in die Finsternis* [*Severin's Journey into the Dark*, 1914]. In the years that followed, the volume was modified to expand its breadth by adding short prose, an unpublished "Golem-drama," and a few selected poems. The title of this new collection was to be *Der Enkel des Golem* [The Golem's Grandson]. Yet this collection also never materialized. Instead, it was reduced solely to the still unpublished novel *Blaugast*, which finally came out in 1984.

This edition was a reprint of the novel found in volume

IV of my 1973 dissertation on Paul Leppin. The text is taken from the two identical carbon copies of the typescript. Both copies have the same handwritten emendations made by Leppin, except one contains a few marks in the margin and cuts that to me seem to have been clearly made by someone else, most likely an editor. The main difference between the two copies is the title page: one had the title "Der Untergang," and it was struck through in red pencil and changed to "Blaugast." The subtitle on this copy is "Roman eines Besessenen" [A Novel of One Obsessed]. The second copy has a title page of heavier paper and it reads: "Blaugast. Roman eines Untergangs." [Blaugast: A Novel of Decline]. With the 1984 edition, I tried to present the text as close as possible to Leppin's last intentions and disregarded the text cuts, which looked to me like censorship, and I gave it the title that appeared in 1938 in *Prager Rhapsodie* as forthcoming: *Blaugast. Ein Roman aus dem alten Prag* [Blaugast: A Novel from Old Prague].

It should be mentioned that three of the novel's eighteen chapters had been previously published as stories in their own right: in 1920 the magazine *Das Riff* ran chapter XI as "Die Vergeltung" ["Retribution"], which was also included the same year in the collection *Das Paradies der Andern* [*Others' Paradise*]; chapters VIII and IX were printed separately in 1928 as *Rede der Kindesmörderin vor dem*

Weltgericht [The Defense of the Child Murderess at the Last Judgment].

, *Blaugast* was the first new publication of Leppin's work since his death in 1945, and though its readership was limited, it sparked new interest in his work. A reprint of *Daniel Jesus* appeared in 1986, albeit nothing more than an underground publication, an insert in a youth magazine (official republication had to wait until 2001). Likewise, the first new anthology of short prose and poems, *Eine Alt-Prager Rhapsodie* (1985), with illustrations by Karel Trinkewitz, was a private print. It took another five years for a modified version to be made available in bookshops, now bearing the title *Alt-Prager Spaziergänge* [Strolls through Old Prague, 1990] and containing historical photos selected by Pavel Scheufler. *Der Gefangene* [The Prisoner], a volume of poems collected from the manuscripts in the Strahov and Marbach archives, and a reprint of Leppin's best-known work, *Severin's Journey into the Dark*, were both published in 1988. It was the year the *Prager Presse* had predicted in 1938, honoring Leppin's sixtieth birthday, that he would find renewed fame:

> Poets, real poets, do not live for their own life; they do not live for their contemporaries. Much later someone will open a forgotten slim volume, and the doors of life will open up for both: the silent speaker and the silent listener. It is not fame that descends but something

more elevated: immortality. Paul Leppin's verse awaits its readers in 1988.

In some ways perhaps the prediction was correct, because the decade following the fall of communism in 1989 resulted in the publication of many new editions and translations, particularly in his native city where Czech translations of both *Daniel Jesus* and *Severin's Journey* (which had circulated in samizdat) appeared in the early 1990s. Several further volumes are in preparation as are two short films in English. Among the re-editions to appear in German are the novel *Hüter der Freude* [The Hedonist, 1918] and, most importantly, the first of the five volumes of Leppin's collected work: *Dreizehn Kapitel Liebe aus der Hölle* [Thirteen Chapters a Love from Hell], with illustrations from Oscar-winning artist H.R. Giger.

* * *

There is little doubt that Leppin's work is essential to an understanding of the literary and cultural situation in Prague during the first decades of the 20th century. In his sexual imagery, Leppin captures the sociological and cultural circumstances of the time and place from an outsider's perspective, and feelings of isolation and confronting "the other" are central to his work. In Prague, all were outsiders in their own ways as all found themselves isolated: the Germans were a minority; the Czechs were socially oppressed; the Jews were the epitome of the outsider. The cultural complexity of the city found expression in the heated debates that were current among the city's intellectuals about existing ghettos and how to negate such divisions. Leppin's work is an important piece of the mosaic because it is saturated with the atmosphere of Prague. He often mentioned his relationship to the city in his correspondence, and it echoed Kafka's famous statement that Prague was a "mother with claws" from which one could hardly escape. Indeed, to his fiancée, Henriette Bogner, he wrote in 1907: "You know, it is a strange feeling; I cannot stand [Prague], almost to the point of hatred. But then there are moments when I feel a deep love for Prague and would be truly sad if I ever had to leave it." This proved prophetic as contrary to Henriette's expectations that they would live in Vienna after they were married, Leppin could not tear himself away from his home, and they lived in the upscale Vinohrady district until his death.

Leppin's oeuvre should also be seen in the context of the evolving scientific field of sexology. From the beginning of his literary career around 1900, his work addressed the role of sexuality for the individual, "the distress and the anxiety of men and women tortured by the agony of sexuality," as he explained in defense of *Daniel Jesus* (whose centerpiece, a masked ball, became part of Arthur Schnitzler's *Dream Story* (1926) and hence a key element in Stanley Kubrick's 1999 film *Eyes Wide Shut*). The year *Daniel Jesus* was published, 1905, is also the year of Sigmund Freud's *Three Essays on the Theory of Sexuality*. In addition to Freud, the studies of Richard von Krafft-Ebing (*Psychopathia Sexualis*, 1886), Havelock Ellis (*Studies in Psychology of Sex*, 1897), Otto Weininger (*Sex and Character*, 1903), August Forel (*The Sexual Question*, 1906) and others were widely discussed in intellectual circles. The most striking example in *Blaugast* is Chapter XVI, likely a direct reference to Krafft-Ebing's case 232 (14th edition, ed. Alfred Fuchs):

> M, sixty years of age, owner of several millions, happily married, father of two daughters, one eighteen, the other sixteen years of age, was [...] accustomed to go to the house of a procuress, where he was known as "the prick-man," and there, lying upon a sofa in a pink silk dressing-gown, lavishly trimmed with lace, would await his victims — three nude girls. They had to approach him in single file, in silence and smiling. They gave him needles, cambric handkerchiefs and a whip. Kneeling before one of the girls, he would now stick about a hundred needles in her body, and fasten with twenty needles a handkerchief upon her bosom; this he would suddenly tear away, whip the girl, tear the hair from

her mons veneris and squeeze her breasts, etc., whilst the other two girls would wipe the perspiration from his forehead and strike lascivious attitudes. Now excited to the highest pitch, he would have coitus with his victim.*

As Krafft-Ebing is responsible for Leopold von Sacher-Masoch's name being remembered more for the term "masochism" than for his novels, he might very well have coined the term "leppinism" for the sexual obsession of dressing up and acting out scenes (such as in chapter V or in Leppin's play *Der blaue Zirkus* [The Blue Circus, 1928]). Sacher-Masoch's *Venus in Furs* was very much part of these discussions about sexology during Leppin's time and it was a direct influence on both *Severin's Journey* and Kafka's *The Metamorphosis*.

There was a vibrant exchange of ideas between the various cultural centers, and the many artists and writers who participated and played crucial roles in their time are largely forgotten today. One was Otto Gross — the sex guru of Monte Verità, Ascona circa 1905, a " 'paradise seeker' between Freud and Jung," as his biographer Emanuel Hurwitz referred to him. Gross was one of the first defenders of Freud's theories, and his father was the famous criminologist Hans Gross, who as a teacher had an influence

---

*Richard von Krafft-Ebing, *Psychopathia Sexualis: The Case Histories* (London: Creation Books, 2000) 234-235, where it is listed as case 220.

on Kafka's work (e.g., "In the Penal Colony"). Otto Gross revived not only the ideas of Johann Jakob Bachofen's *Mother Right,* but became the spokesman of love's intrinsic beauty and the champion of the free love found in D. H. Lawrence's work. (Lawrence's future wife, Frieda von Richthofen, had been "liberated" by Gross before she got to know and eventually marry the English poet.) There are parallels between Lawrence's definition of pornography in *Pornography and Obscenity* (1929), as that which depicts sexuality as sinful and despicable rather than beautiful and sacred, and the views Leppin expressed in his collection of essays *Venus auf Abwegen* [Venus Astray, 1920]. Both saw the bourgeoisie, the "defenders" of morality, as the actual creators of pornography. Hypocritically denying sexuality in their "normal" life, the bourgeois male then uses prostitutes to live out his sexual desires and thereby degrades women to the role of sex slave.

Chapters VIII and IX of *Blaugast* summarize, in an extremely powerful and condensed form, Leppin's accusations against a world where utilitarian norms dominate basic human needs and values. The novel is a revolt against an ideology of altruism, which Leppin exposes as masked egotism. Morality so-called is a strategy employed by the establishment for their self-protection, and by those who profit from maintaining these social norms. Seeing themselves in the role of judges who condemn the depraved, their "humanistic" self-deception looks down on the "morally corrupt," the outcasts. In *Blaugast*, the whore who loved the child she has murdered poses the question: "Do you know what a life such as mine looks like? Gagged, ravished, always in the mud, in the gutter, in darkness? Oh, no. You don't. You sat in your offices, rubbed your bellies against impressive desks, your thoughts stewing in the thick juice of boredom."

Leppin had no sentimental illusions about prostitution and was very much aware of its social implications. He neither depicted it as a profession of choice, nor as the dream job of the sexually obsessed female. On the contrary, he recognized the humiliation, the pain and suffering, the loneliness, hopelessness and injustice this life entailed. But he also knew that humaneness and altruism were more often found in this world of poverty than anywhere else. "I think that all of us are human beings. I think no one is better than the other," he once remarked in a letter to Henriette decades before writing *Blaugast*. This very fundamental assumption was the basis for his life and his work: in both the early *Berg der Erlösung* [Mountain of Redemption, 1908] and *Blaugast*, it is the outcast who delivers salvation.

Although the popular portrayal of prostitutes as saints

is somewhat a literary cliché, Leppin was not put off from making use of it. Both Berta Wieland in *Mountain of Redemption* and Johanna in *Blaugast* represent the archetypal prostitute with a heart of gold, the altruistic whore sacrificing herself for others, understanding the needs of others and trying to save them. They are the "*meretrix dolorosa*," the suffering harlots, as Eisner described Leppin's women, "queens of the soul in exile, Magdalenes beaten down by the original sin of the world." Harsh, realistic description is juxtaposed against religious, illusionary imagery. The obscure intermingles with the pious — a duality Brod clearly discerned in Leppin when he called him a *poeta religiosus*. In his comments on *Blaugast* he noted:

> . . . the opera glasses with which [Leppin] looks at the scenery of the world have two different lenses. One is very precise and shows everything in unrelenting realism; the other one seems to be made of frosted topaz or a soft, rose-colored fog. Depending whether he looks through the left or right lens, his landscape, his scenery appears as villainous, rotten, roguish — or enraptured, delightful, tinkling with the sound of music boxes. Drastic contrasts that alternate from one second to the next. Out of the twilight and terrifying, brooding thunderclouds flashes the halo of purifying lightning.

Leppin was always true to himself in both life and art.

He did what he thought he should do without weighing the consequences. He was never an opportunist; in fact, he was just the opposite. He opposed the traditionalists when he was young and experienced isolation as a result. When he tackled the burden of sexuality, he was well aware that he would be accused of pornography, as Egon Schiele had been in Vienna for his drawings of nudes. Leppin did not succumb to fascism, nor did he betray his friends when he was subjected to interrogation and incarceration as an old man. He did not write with the literary critics and his standing in intellectual circles in mind, although he was more than familiar with the politics and trends of the art world. True to character, he did not avoid kitsch if he thought it necessary to express a truth, his truth. As he explained:

> Kitsch, painted a gaudy gold, hung with trinkets and glitter, people should not despise you. You are able to comfort widows and give warmth to those who are freezing; you are a friend to those in mourning; you are able to release the most precious gifts people possess: respect and tears. You are the stepsister of art whose name is written on the banner that is carried in the campaigns against you. You are corrupt, degenerate, a failure; but you are from the same land as art: from the neighboring regions of heaven.

Leppin's approach to writing was neither analytic nor

metaphoric in the traditional sense, and he did not create webs of intertextual and intellectual references. For him, emotions were the key to effective literature. The depiction of atmosphere, not plot, characterizes all his works, as critics and admirers have noted again and again. The poet Wilhelm von Scholz remarked in 1902: "It seems to me that next to Rainer Maria Rilke, Paul Leppin is the finest depicter of sentiment among the young German Bohemians," and in 1914 the Czech literary historian Arne Novák called him a "virtuoso of alluring nocturnes." The artist Alfred Kubin, whose yearning for Prague was awakened by Leppin's books, spoke of "intuitively and intimately conceived pictures [...] of this quite strange city whose undercurrents are magically unveiled," while Mathias Schnitzler, a young reviewer of the recent German edition of *Daniel Jesus* observed correctly that the novel is an "adventure" filled with images that would reappear about fifteen years later in films such as *The Cabinet of Dr. Caligari* (1919). The intense atmosphere and the emotions of Leppin's characters, whose experience is an amalgam of pleasure and pain, almost cause the covers of his books to explode.

Otto Pick, one of Prague's influential editors, journalists, and translators, wrote in a letter to Leppin in 1933 after having read *Blaugast* in manuscript: "I have just finished reading the last pages of your novel, which is no novel but something almost unique in our time, the present time: a powerful and pure piece of poetry [...] that has been *genuinely and painfully experienced up to its last detail.*"

Leppin's writing was indeed something new, something provocative in German literature, and I would wager that with hindsight future studies will demonstrate his work to have been crucial for this literature on its way toward modernity. Located at the crossroads between East and West, Leppin, as M. Schnitzler notes, "pointed the way for German literature from Art-Nouveau decadence to the expressionistic scream." Stanislaw Przybyszewski, Charles Baudelaire, Joris-Karl Huysmans, Théophile Gautier, and Jiří Karásek ze Lvovic are among Leppin's soul mates, while Kafka is generally considered by critics to be his stylistic opposite. While Kafka is lauded for his objectivity and restraint, Leppin is accused of hyberbole and excess by scholars such as Klaus Wagenbach. Closer scrutiny will reveal that this black-and-white dichotomy does neither writer justice and that there may be a common "Prague language" based on common experience. Both, each in their own way, were innovators.

In *Blaugast,* the everyday world and the realm of shadows, fears, and anxieties merge. Boundaries dissolve, objects become animate, and the pragmatic use of language breaks down. Sounds and connotations influence the flow of words and sentences. Images of rats, pus, sores, and excrement evoke disgust. Such images either compels the reader to throw the book to the floor or become sucked into its world, a world that men and women have turned into a hell for one another. Just a tiny flicker of hope is all that remains. Sometimes, it just may happen that a character reaches out, that someone understands rather than accuses, that life's confusion is overcome and a transcendental harmony achieved.

Dierk O. Hoffmann, 2007

Translator's Note

As has so often been stated, Prague for many centuries had been a city of three peoples: the Czechs, the Germans and the Jews. "Prague German" as a dialect or mode can be traced to the early 14th century, and the era of the unique literature that employed it was effectively over with the Second World War. We are thus left with a finite amount of Prague German literature, much of which, however, has been wholly untouched by translators and literary scholars.

As a member of the German-speaking minority of Prague, Leppin's language presents unique challenges to the translator. Johannes Urzidil once referred to the German of his native city as "cut off from development in the static diaspora of the Czech milieu . . . a 'Sunday best' German [that] any 'learned gentleman in Berlin' would have . . . declared *dead*."* Lenka Reinerová, who is the last living

*In Peter Demetz, "Noch einmal: Prager Deutsch." [One More Time: Prague German] *Literature und Kritik*, vol 1, issue 6: 58. Translations from German are my own.

Prague German writer, has stated that rather than a dialect, it is a "tint" that reflects the atmosphere of Prague. Of course, if one were to identify variants then one would have to define what constitutes the "pure" core. It is perhaps more productive to look at how well Prague Germans actually grasped what could be called "the highest of Hochdeutsch [Standard German]." According to Peter Demetz, who grew up speaking Prague German: "This language is 'pure' (metaphorically speaking) in dialect and regional color, but with all of its adopted Slavisms in no way is it a 'pure Standard German.'"*

Any translator without a working knowledge of Czech will likely find it difficult to penetrate the unique nature of this Prague German "tint": Austrian regional dictionaries offer little help and Prague German dictionaries simply do not exist. Instead, one must familiarize oneself with Czech terms that are, as is the case in *Blaugast*, Germanized — *Pawelatsch*, for example, which I have translated as "veranda," comes from the Czech *pavlač*, a balcony-like gallery found in the interior courtyards of many Prague apartment buildings — or appear in the original Czech, like *maminka*, the term of endearment for "mother," rather than the standard German diminutive *Mütterchen*. And many times Czech syntax is replicated as well.

Ibid, 59.

In addition, Leppin's writing has its own peculiarities. In *Blaugast* we find strings of adjectival constructions within elongated sentences structures, lexical fugues (e.g., military and commercial terms) extending, even belaboring, metaphor. He was prone to hyper-stylized flourishes and inventing words ("Leppinisms"): *Mottenzauber* in chapter XIV, which I have translated as "moth-beguiling," to describe the shabby costumes in Schobotzki's shop; *Blutrauch*, or "blood-colored smoke," in chapter XIII describes the heartbreaking emotions Johanna experiences as her mother lay dying of syphilis. Leppin also molded the language in an effort to express wild visions and violent dreams. Similar to stream-of-consciousness writing, his sentences are often devoid of relative pronouns and display a lack of cohesion, which makes determining connotation and meaning especially problematic. Yet it is a style that set him apart from other Prague German writers of his day, such as Franz Kafka or Hermann Ungar, both of whom intentionally pared down their prose. I have attempted to render this style in an English that, while making concessions to intelligibility, I hope retains Leppin's original rhythms as well as the linguistic play of his voice. Therefore, mythological terms such as *Seifentier* and *Pompuwa*, which have no English equivalents, remain here in the original without unwieldy explanation.

Similarly, the fact of Leppin's illness itself, its inexorable advance as *Blaugast* was being written, posed yet another challenge. Given that his neurological system was attacked, I had to make the assumption that some of his phrasings and word choices were products of his illness. Yet Leppin also ingeniously uses language to delve deeper into the syphilitic mind, his mind, assaulting the reader with a steady swill of blasphemous images, a progression of corrupt and depraved behavior. His complex "painting" with language resulted in my having first to unravel textual entanglements before reassembling them in translation, conveying his images, dreams and visions by rerouting words, patching in relative clauses, and being inventive with syntax. If subject-pronoun agreement seems tenuous in places — a particular problem that pops up several times in the novel — this is how it appears in the original. It is my opinion that these apparent "mistakes" reflect Leppin's state of mind at the time of the novel's writing, and to fix them as I saw fit would make the translation an untrue representative of this fact as well as a disservice to the text. I have tried to keep the translation as true as possible to the original.

These contortions of language reflecting the contortions of body and mind is one of the more remarkable aspects of the novel, a device for Leppin's masterful description of the ravishes of syphilis in both its internal filthiness and the ugliness of its outward symptoms (Blaugast's twisted body, deformed from the onslaught of the disease). Likewise, grotesque episodes in general are plentiful: Blaugast's imitation of a giant bird, and then masturbating onto a plate; Schobotzki's resemblance to a bird of prey; the obscene playacting in Blaugast's apartment; the fat bourgeois of the beer gardens, food splattered on their shirts, vulgar in their joviality — "sinister buffoonery" it has been called in reference to Fyodor Sologub.* And it is Schobotzki's costume shop that highlights the general mayhem. His strange collection of assorted disguises allows people to transform themselves into either creatures of beauty (in direct opposition to their true appearance) or distorted and vile creatures. Behind a mask one loses the inhibition to commit perverse or indecent acts, as well as the fear of retribution.

Blaugast can be located within the broad stream of fin-de-siècle Decadence. Completed in the 1930s, it is a stylized portrayal of the decadent sensibility confronting modernity (with a final nod to Futurism), and when compared to the works of the interwar avant-garde, it might come across as something of an anachronism, the fruit of a late Decadence decades after the movement's advent (it is not only the last Decadent Prague novel, but likely the last such novel from

*Linda Jean Ivanits, "The Grotesque in F.K. Sologub's Novel *The Petty Demon*," Dissertation (unpublished), University of Wisconsin Madison, 1973: 30.

Central Europe). The general themes of eroticism, absurdity, beauty's decay, the apparent infatuation with the self connect it to an entire corpus of Decadent literature. Indeed, the lineaments of Sologub's *The Petty Demon* (1907), as evidenced by the character of Peredonov, can be seen coursing through it:

> His sensibilities were dull and his consciousness was an apparatus for corruption and destruction. Everything that reached his consciousness was transformed into something vile and filthy. He was immediately taken with deformities in objects and he rejoiced over them. Whenever he passed an erect and pure column, he wanted to deform it or deface it. He laughed with joy when things were spoiled in his presence.*

The moral decay Peredonov so admires resonantes in Blaugast's exhibitionism in parks and public displays of sexual gratification.

In truth, a novel such as *Blaugast* poses an enormous challenge for any translator. Conveying subtleties of meaning or word play from a dialect that is, for the most part, defunct only makes the task that more daunting. I have attempted to retain the emotion and the intricacies of style

---

*Fyodor Sologub, *The Petty Demon*, translated by S. D. Cioran (Ann Arbor: Ardis, 1983) 97.

to the best of my abilities, and any errors or false perceptions are entirely my own.

This translation would not have been made possible without the assistance of many individuals and organizations, who graciously supported me throughout this effort. Many thanks to Dr. Dierk Hoffmann, whose vast knowledge of Leppin, his psyche and his language, proved invaluable to me when interpreting his shades of meaning. A sabbatical leave approved by the Department of Foreign Languages and Literatures and the SUNY-Geneseo College Administration provided me the needed time to devote myself to the endeavor. ACTR/ACCELS of Washington, D.C. and the Geneseo Research Council also provided me with generous grants for support of my work with my editor, Howard Sidenberg, in Prague. I have him as well as Graham Hettlinger of ACTR/ACCELS and Joshua Cohen to thank for their efforts and assistance. No such work is possible, however, without the aid of great libraries and tireless librarians. I thank Geneseo College's Milne Library, especially Interlibrary Loan and the National Library in Prague, especially my librarian friend, PhDr. Františka Vrbenská, the Museum of Czech Literature, and the Jewish Museum in Prague. Countless hours of translating were made possible by the company of fine friends in my off-time: Klára Černušáková, Michaela Hájková, Alisa Mayor and Petr

Pajdlhauser, who offered me a great place to stay in Prague while I worked. Lastly, James Bonney, whose excellent eye and professional knowledge of English syntax assisted me in creating a readable work. It is due to his support and easygoing nature that this work was completed.

Cynthia A. Klima, 2007

About the Author

Paul Leppin was born in Prague on November 27, 1878, the second son of Josef Leppin and Pauline Scharsach. Both were from Friedland, in Moravia, and had come to Prague just before their marriage hoping to improve their social situation in the city through the many opportunities not available in the provinces. She was a teacher, he a clockmaker, a profession he had to abandon to clerk in a law office while his wife cared for their two sons. Forced by the economic difficulties of his family to forgo a university education, Leppin entered the civil service soon after graduating from Gymnasium, working as an accountant for the Telegraph and Postal Service until he retired for health reasons. It was here that he witnessed firsthand the life-numbing existence of his contemporaries, a theme that consistently made its way into his writing.

Beginning with the novella *The Doors of Life* in 1901, Leppin's poetry, prose, and essays appeared regularly in Prague and Germany over the next four decades. In contrast to his staid professional life, Leppin's literary career was marked by a desire to "shock the bourgeois," which earned him the unofficial title "king of Prague bohemians." Famous for his mischievous songs, his love of parties, his organizational talent as well as his decadent lifestyle, he became the leading figure of a young generation of Prague German artists during the first decade of the 20th century. Known as Jung-Prag [Young Prague], they congregated around the two literary publications Leppin edited, *Frühling* [Spring] and *Wir* [We], and sought to combat the city's cultural provincialism typified by the conservative Concordia group.

While Leppin's name was becoming known outside of Prague, he was often subject to attacks at home. His novel *Daniel Jesus* was lauded by the Expressionists in Berlin, yet condemned as pornography in Prague. His railing at the city's literary establishment in the pages of *Wir* eventually damaged his own future career, and the publication had to fold after only two issues. Indeed, *Wir* was the last attempt by the group to gain an audience, and most associated with it would eventually leave Prague. Leppin was one of the few to stay. He married Henriette Bogner in 1907, and her wish to move to the chic metropolis of Vienna was unable to break the hold Leppin's native city had on him. The Vinohrady district — Prag-Weinberge as he knew it growing up — remained their home.

Leppin once commented that he hoped the revolutionary gestures of his group and the rejection they had endured would at least benefit a younger generation of writers coalescing around Franz Kafka and Max Brod, who considered him "the chosen bard of the painfully disappearing old Prague." In Leppin's own words, he was "a monument to times past," the last representative of an era. He continued to write novels, plays (performed at the Neues Deutsches Theater), stories, and poems — Prague always forming a strong influence — and he became secretary of the Union of

German Writers in Czechoslovakia, which had been founded by Oskar Baum and Johannes Urzidil.

Leppin, in fact, was one of the few German writers to have close contacts with contemporary Czech artists and writers. He translated Czech poetry and wrote articles on Czech literature and art for German periodicals, and had his own work published in *Moderní revue*, the main organ of Czech Decadence. Serving as a mediator between the cultures, he "set an example as poet and as citizen that a fruitful and peaceful coexistence of both nationalities (Czech and German) is possible in one state without having to give up one's national identity," as Otto Pick remarked in an address given on Leppin's 50th birthday. His contribution to the city's literature and culture was recognized both in 1934, when he was awarded the Schiller Memorial Prize, and in 1938, when on his 60th birthday he received an Honorary Recognition for Writers from the Czechoslovak Ministry of Culture. In the same year, two volumes of his *Prager Rhapsodie* appeared (a collection of poetry and short prose illustrated by Hugo Steiner-Prag), marking the end of his publishing activity.

The remaining years of Leppin's life were a living hell. After the German occupation of Prague in March 1939, he was temporarily detained and interrogated by the Gestapo. He never learned the reason for it, but most likely he had been denounced as a Jew. Some literary historians did indeed consider him a Jewish writer, and his scandalous books and his good relations with both Czech and Jewish artists provided additional proof that he belonged to a group that undermined Aryan values. Another reason might have been the refusal by the Union of German Writers in Czechoslovakia under his leadership to join the Nazi sponsored Literary Society of Germany. Whatever the case, his poor physical and psychological state — a result of an advanced syphilis and a stroke suffered shortly after his release from Pankrac Prison — rapidly deteriorated and left him utterly helpless in the years to come. The Union was dissolved by the Nazi authorities, and Leppin made a futile attempt to obtain a party membership card in order to receive medical care. He sat in a wheelchair most of the day being looked after by his wife and waiting for the visits of Marianne von Hoop, a young friend who brought him medication to relieve his pain (her husband was a physician). She also understood how to get his mind off his suffering and was able to motivate him to write again: a cycle of poems, *Der Gefangene* [The Prisoner], and a novella, *Monika. Dreizehn Kapitel Liebe aus der Hölle* [Monika: Thirteen Chapters a Love from Hell], which he completed at the end of 1944. These were his last works.

Leppin died, virtually forgotten, just before midnight on April 10, 1945. He is buried in Prague's Vinohrady Cemetery.

About the Contributors

Cynthia A. Klima is Associate Professor of German, Slavic and Humanities at State University of New York: College at Geneseo. She is a regular contributor to various journals and anthologies.

Dierk O. Hoffmann is Professor of German at Colgate University. He is the editor of Paul Leppin's complete works and has contributed the volume on *Der Rosenkavalier* to the multi-volume critical edition of Hugo von Hofmannsthal's collected works.

BLAUGAST
A Novel of Decline
by Paul Leppin

Translated from the German by Cynthia A. Klima
Edited by Joshua Cohen
Original typescript in the literary archives of the Museum of Czech
Literature, whose assistance we gratefully acknowledge.
Originally published in German as
Blaugast: Ein Roman aus dem alten Prag in 1984 by Langen-Müller
Bibliothek, Munich, edited by Dirk O. Hoffmann.
Cover photograph by František Drtikol, reprinted by
permission of the Museum of Decorative Arts in Prague.
Text set in Garamond Semibold
Design by J. Slast

First edition published in 2007 by
TWISTED SPOON PRESS
P.O. Box 21 — Preslova 12
150 21 Prague 5, Czech Republic
www.twistedspoon.com

Printed and bound in the Czech Republic
by PB Tisk, Příbram

Distributed to the trade by
SCB DISTRIBUTORS
15608 South New Century Drive
Gardena, CA 90248-2129, USA
www.scbdistributors.com

CENTRAL BOOKS
99 Wallis Road
London, E9 5LN, UK
www.centralbooks.com